Michael Bruce, William Stephen

Poetical Works of Michael Bruce

Michael Bruce, William Stephen

Poetical Works of Michael Bruce

ISBN/EAN: 9783742814517

Manufactured in Europe, USA, Canada, Australia, Japa

Cover: Foto ©Andreas Hilbeck / pixelio.de

Manufactured and distributed by brebook publishing software
(www.brebook.com)

Michael Bruce, William Stephen

Poetical Works of Michael Bruce

THE POETICAL WORKS

OF

MICHAEL BRUCE

WITH LIFE AND WRITINGS

BY

Rev. WILLIAM STEPHEN.

KELTY, BLAIR ADAM.

J. AND R. PARLANE, PAISLEY.

JOHN MENZIES AND CO., EDINBURGH AND GLASGOW.

HOULSTON AND SONS, LONDON.

1895.

PREFACE.

No account need here be given of how this service, on behalf of Michael Bruce and his admirers, came to assume its present form. Instead of a brief monograph, on the Poet and his Writings, I have been induced to undertake an edition of the Poems to which this now forms the introduction.

It has been suggested that the time is highly opportune for a new edition of Michael Bruce. Having resided for a considerable period of my life in near vicinity to the scenes now indissolubly linked with the name of the Poet of Lochleven, and having also had opportunities of intercourse with those best acquainted with the subject in the district and elsewhere, I have been led to familiarize myself with the invaluable Works of Dr MacKelvie and Dr Grosart, and generally with the Bruce, and the Bruce-Logan literature and controversy.

How far the result of these somewhat desultory studies may appear to warrant its publication, in endeavouring to bring out a new and popular edition of these Poems, it is not for me to say.

What friendly help or encouragement I have received from any quarter, in prosecuting my task, I gladly acknowledge. In particular let me convey my thanks to Mr David Marshall, F.S.A. Scot., one of the foremost of our antiquarian authorities on matters pertaining to Kinross, for giving me the benefit of his extensive knowledge on this subject, and for his courtesy in placing at my disposal some rare and valuable books for consultation in my studies.

The retracing of the pathetic yet ever inspiring life-story of Michael Bruce, and the cultivation of a somewhat closer acquaintance with his works, have been to me anything but uncongenial tasks. If I shall have the still further satisfaction of imparting something of this pleasure, and I trust profit, to others who may read the book, I shall consider that my services, in such a cause, have been abundantly rewarded.

W. S.

F.C. MANSE, KELTY,
BLAIR ADAM, 1895.

Life.

O Truth ! O Freedom ! how are ye still born
  In the rude stable, in the manger nursed !
What humble hands unbar those gates of morn
  Through which the splendours of the New-Day burst !

—Lowell.

MICHAEL BRUCE.

I.

LIFE.

THERE is no finer view of the County of Kinross than that which can be obtained, on a clear summer or autumn day, from the summit of Benarty, a little to the north of the old Roman camp. Sheridan's well-known impromptu might be varied somewhat thus to suit the situation :—

> "How pleasant, away from the turmoil of party,
> To look out on Kinross from the brow of Benarty !"

Right beneath this point of view lies Lochleven, embosomed in the vale of Kinross. Though not by any means the largest of our Scottish lakes, it is among the most picturesque, and by far the richest of them all in historical associations. A little to the east, is the island of St. Serf and his Culdees, bleak and bare enough as it meets the eye. That venerable monastic ruin, dating in its original from the close of the eighth century, and next in order of time after Iona, among our Culdee settlements, is itself a memorial to the honour of Brude V., the last of the Pictish kings, whose gift it was to St. Serf and his followers. Here, for long centuries, was one of the chiefest sanctuaries of the Christian faith in Scotland, and those heaving mounds around are what remains of the cells and graves of our earliest Scottish missionaries. Here, in the fifteenth century, Wyntoun, the then Prior of St. Serf's, composed the "Cronykil of Scotland."

Can we wonder that a spot so sacred should have been long, by common consent, revered as one of the shrines of our country ?

Further to the west, rising over the waters, is another and much smaller island, on which upstands the massive keep of "High Lochleven Castle" with its old world record of royal residence, of heroic struggles, chiefly with the Southron, and of dreary state imprisonments. The supreme interest which, in more modern times, attaches to Lochleven Castle, is its connection with the declining fortunes of the ill-fated Mary Stuart. Within it the unhappy Scottish queen spent the first and only year among her own subjects of her long and cruel captivity. There, under violent constraint, she had to stoop to sign away her claim to the throne of Scotland. There also was enacted the exciting drama of her escape, only that she might fall at last into the fatal grasp of her sworn enemy Elizabeth.

The lake-girt prison-house of Mary Stuart is thus another of our Scottish shrines whither the devotee frequently resorts.

Westward, and now landward, we descry the Mansion House of Blair Adam, with its prettily wooded policies, favourite haunts of Sir Walter Scott during his frequent visits, while a member of the Blair Adam Antiquarian Club.

Further north and further west we can see the weird form of Dowhill Castle, where, still keeping loyal vigil, the ghost of Lindsay is not yet laid. Still further to the west and north of the county may be noted the sites of old baronial castles, each with its own distinctive history. and rising sentinel-like in view of Lochleven.

The town of Kinross, "whose stately tufted groves nod o'er the lake," lives in the midst of, and to some extent upon, these ancient glories of its surroundings, and from the vantage ground of our Benarty outlook we can see it life size.

But our immediate concern is with the north-east end of this panorama, known, from ancient times, as Bishopshire, but perhaps still more widely as the parish of Portmoak. The parish is rich in relics, sacred and secular, of the olden times. It has also, through its temporary connection with the Erskines, a prominent place in the ecclesiastical history of our country during the last century. The prevailing character of the locality is, however, that of retirement and repose.

In this quiet, slow-moving region, even in these bustling modern days, we alight, in our survey, from our mount of vision, on the birthplace, and near it the last resting-place. of Michael Bruce—the nobly gifted poet of Kinross.

Such are some of the more prominent features of the locality which owes so much of its celebrity to the piety and genius of its youthful poet.

There is a manifest harmony between the outer and the inner world in which Bruce lived and died, so far at least as such a true genius as his can ever permit its owner to die. The lyre of Bruce is not yet unstrung, its chords are still swept beneath the shelter of the Lomonds ; and the minstrel, modest and retiring as he was, is not, and cannot be, forgotten.

The visitor to Portmoak is soon made aware, if at all sensitive to such impressions, of the spell which Bruce still continues to cast over the minds of the more intelligent of its inhabitants.

But it is not alone in Portmoak or its neighbourhood that the magic spell of Bruce's genius exerts its potency.

Our business, in these pages, is, in the hope of somewhat extending that influence, to give a brief sketch of his life, and then an estimate of his writings.

The life of Michael Bruce was not written by the man who edited the first edition of his poems, and who, of all others, one might suppose, had both the materials and qualifications for rendering this sacred service to his friend, whose literary executor he had voluntarily constituted himself. Whether this omission was or was not an advantage, we need not enquire. What Logan his first editor did, was simply to prefix a brief paragraph or two of high-flown eulogy, and for the rest, to leave the touching story of that winsome life altogether untold. Nay more, however the literary controversy, which shall be considered in its place, may be settled, no one ventures to deny that Logan lost or destroyed the MSS. both of the poems and letters, from which another might have constructed a worthy record. The few letters of Bruce which have been preserved give us some idea of the serious character of this mishap. It is not more true that Bruce was possessed of the highest poetic genius, than it is that he excelled as a master of the epistolary style of writing. He makes frequent and always happy references to himself in his letters, and delights in laying bare his heart to a sympathetic correspondent.

Sketches of Bruce did appear ; one by his friend David Pearson,[1] another by Lord Craig in the "Mirror" for the year 1779, and one by Dr Anderson in his "British Poets." The number gradually increased, and it by-and-bye became fashionable to give Bruce a place among the acknowledged stars in the firmament of letters. We do not profess to even enumerate the chief works bearing on Bruce and his literary claims, which are now accessible to every student. The new era in the posthumous fame of Bruce dates from the appearance of Dr MacKelvie's great work, entitled, "Lochleven and other Poems by Michael Bruce. With a life of the author from original sources (1837)." With this publication, the Logan–Bruce controversy was at last launched in due form, and it has been taken up with great ardour on both sides.

[1] The sketch referred to is found among the Baird MSS., and is entitled "A few Memorials of the Life of Mr Michael Bruce." The entire sketch appears in Dr J. Small's article in *British and Foreign Evangelical Review*, 1877—on "Michael Bruce and the Authorship of the Ode to the Cuckoo." The following extract proves that Bruce had a considerable circle of correspondents, and indicates their estimate of him as a letter writer. "From this place (*i.e.*, Gairney Bridge), and from the University, he wrote many letters to his friends, particularly Mr Arnot of Portmoak, to Mrs Dryburgh, Henderson, Lawson, Logan, and to myself, which I shall ever esteem. I reckon them a part of my treasure. Alas! from the excess of my veneration for them I carried them about with me till they were sore wasted and some of them lost, besides what I lost by Mr Logan, who never returned those he received, nor yet the finished copy of his poems, which he got at the same time from his father. As an epistolary writer he was truly excellent ; and here allow me to insert the sentiments of a learned lady, Mrs Keir, upon this very thing. In a letter to Mr Hervey she says, "One feature of the amiable person they (viz. the letters) exhibit, I contemplate with peculiar delight. I mean the delicacy which originates from a pure heart, a correct taste, and a regulated imagination."

Dr Grosart's edition of Bruce's Works did not see the light until 1865, and is, to a great extent, a restatement of the case of his predecessor. Both biographers were competent, in the highest degree, for their task, but both, and, of course, especially the latter, had the disadvantage of arguing their case on very different data from what would have been available had they, like Logan, belonged to the circle of the poet's personal acquaintances. Dr MacKelvie himself acknowledged that his painstaking work was incomplete, and did not do full justice to the literary claims of Bruce. It was known that he had so far prepared a revised edition, with additional notes, a little before his death ; which, however, somehow seems to have shared a similar fate to the volume of MSS. committed to Logan.

Following such guidance as we have indicated, and such guidance as we have had from a somewhat careful study of the literature generally referred to in Appendix A, p. 61. we shall do our best to give, in the briefest manner, the leading facts in Bruce's life-story, and strive to arrive at some correct idea as to the place he holds in our poetic literature.

Michael Bruce was born in the village of Kinnesswood, on 27th March, 1746. The Christian name of the poet is supposed to have been given him in honour of a noted Covenanting preacher, whose sermons were then widely read in Scotland.[1] The cottage where Bruce was born still continues to draw to Kinnesswood many a visitor of importance, who would not otherwise have discovered the village around which this event has thrown such an abiding lustre in our literary annals. Thus has the humble weaver's dwelling become another of the shrines to which we have referred, as peculiar to Kinross. The home

[1] Grosart, p. 8.

in which Bruce was born and in which he died has been often described.

Dr Huie, in particular, gives a somewhat minute description both of the house and its surroundings, in "The Olive Branch," published in 1831. We can see, in his simple, graphic account, the form of his venerable conductor, John Birrel, then an old man, as he leads the visitor into Bruce's garden.

It is, in truth, a lovely spot, consecrated for all time by memories of piety and genius triumphing over suffering and death. Nothing can well exceed the charm of its striking and finely contrasting surroundings. From this more than royal observatory can be seen, almost at a single glance, the expanse of Lochleven, with the nearer island of Saint Serf, and the far-reaching panorama of hill and dale which makes up the county of Kinross. The heights of "rocky Lomond" form a fitting background to this richly varied scene.

Inside the poet's abode we may well share the involuntary awe with which, Dr Huie tells us, he looked round upon the humble domicile, with its sacred relics and associations. The history of the Kinnesswood cottage is interesting, especially in more recent times. A generation after Dr Huie's visit, Dr Grosart describes it as "a weather worn 'eerie' looking place."

But in 1868, chiefly, if not entirely, by the individual enterprise of two public-spirited men, Mr R. Burns Begg and Mr David Marshall, of Kinross, the fortunes of the fast sinking fabric began to improve. The dwelling was purchased and repaired as a tribute of respect to the memory of the poet. In 1876 was originated the Bruce Memorial Trust, representative of the wide-spread interest in this new movement.

Thus it has come about that the cottage is no longer the

B

"eerie" looking place described by Dr Grosart, but a new and yet old structure, a model of rustic simplicity, and wearing as nearly as possible the same general appearance as it did when the youthful poet reclined in front of it on the grassy mound, "after he became too weak to walk."

Our view shews the cottage, as seen from this point, and as it appears to the visitor of 1895.

Bruce's father and mother must have been above the average of their class, both in intelligence and character. We do not know if we are right in supposing that the typical hand-loom weaver was rather a forward, noisy, if not altogether uncultivated member of society, not a little taken up about his rights and privileges, and having, on such topics, a fluent and forcible delivery. In the class the struggle for life was somewhat absorbing, and repressive of the rapid evolution of what is now known as the altruistic principle. Be this as it may, old Alexander Bruce was eminent for piety and common-sense.[1] He was, at the same time, a modest and reticent man, a man of deeds rather

---

[1] Mr Marshall, in his interesting brochure, "Michael Bruce, a Temperance Reformer," tells us that the poet's father "often amused himself in framing verses," and gives, as a specimen, the following characteristic fragment in the form of an elegy on his gifted son :

"This pious youth early began,
    In morning of his day,
  To seek the Lord his God, that He
    Might teach to him His way.

He did like to young Timothy,
    The Holy Scriptures make
  His frequent study, and in them
    Great pleasure he did take.

For in his childhood he did read
    God's word with special care ;
  And sought the meaning carefully
    Of places dark that were.

He did desire to serve the Lord
    By preaching of His word.
  That by the gospel trumpet he
    His fame might spread abroad :

And publish to the human race
    Glad tidings of good things,
  Which God, in gospel of His grace,
    To guilty sinners brings."

than words. He was an elder in the Secession Church, Milnathort, under the ministry of Thomas Mair, who, along with his large adhering congregation, was ejected from the Anti-Burgher Synod, for holding that "there is a sense in which Christ died for all men." He travelled every Sabbath day, with his family, coming and going to church, a distance of over ten miles. The family was large, consisting of seven, of which Michael was the fifth. Michael was a delicate child. Dr MacKelvie thus describes his appearance when about fourteen years of age :—"He was slenderly made, with a long neck and narrow chest, his skin white and shining ; his cheeks tinged with red rather than ruddy ; his hair yellowish and inclined to curl."[1] From the outset he displayed a vigour and agility of mind which made him at once the prodigy of the village school, and was destined to carry him, almost at a single bound, into the front rank of poetic genius. We have said, almost at a single bound : for we must remember that Michael Bruce had taken the place he holds in our national literature, and was himself laid to rest in the churchyard of Portmoak, before he had much more than completed his twenty-first year. The boy's "pregnant parts" were so manifest that he was, at an early stage, destined to a college course, and, in due time, for the ministry of the Secession Church. Alongside of rapid progress in study we get a glimpse of the boy tending his flock on the slopes of the Lomonds, and drawing inspiration. as we cannot doubt, from his soul-stirring surroundings.

> Love had he found in huts where poor men lie,
> His daily teachers had been woods and rills,
> The silence that is in the starry sky,
> The sleep that is among the lonely hills.

[1] Dr MacKelvie, p. 13.

Bruce, it appears, was a born linguist, and had no trouble in holding the place of dux in his Latin class, when it was his good fortune to be in circumstances to attend the village school. He became, at an early age, a student of Milton and Thomson, and began himself to cultivate the muses. In his classical studies he was fortunate in the village teacher, Mr Dun, and above all he found a noble patron of learning in Mr David Arnot, proprietor of Portmoak, who introduced him to the study of poetry, and with whom he was wont to correspond in Latin. Bruce's schoolfellows in Kinnesswood and early associates were far from commonplace youths. William Arnot, the son of the proprietor at Portmoak, was a kindred genius, as we gather from the poet's description in "Daphnis." Both Pearson and Birrel were men of literary taste if not of learning, and the former was himself a poet.[1]

Bruce was enabled, at last, to enter upon a college life, owing partly to a small legacy coming at this time to his father, a little fortune of something over £11. Afraid of being excluded from St. Andrews College owing to his connection with the Secession Church, he set out for the Edinburgh University in 1762. His student life in Edinburgh unfortunately now remains for us almost a blank. The names of his chief college companions are preserved. They were Mr George Henderson, Mr David Greig, and Mr George Lawson. Two others fall to be added, Mr William Dryburgh, whose "In Memoriam" we have in Philocles; and John Logan, whose name has since come to be so unhappily associated with that of the Kinross poet. One of the literary relics of this period is a letter in which Logan meets some complaint by Dryburgh of his coldness

[1] Dr MacKelvie, p. 19.

in religion, brusquely, by declaring that he considers
" there is no more religion in hearing sermons than there is
iniquity in hearing oaths." Logan, it would seem, had
joined the College Circle as a fervent Seceder, fresh from
the ministry of Rev. John Brown, of Haddington, and
having an eye to becoming, in due time, a minister in the
Burgher connection.

He afterwards, it seems, so cooled down, or, as one of his
biographers puts it, so triumphed over sectarian zeal and
fanaticism, as to go over to the Established Church.
Whatever other vices may have cleaved to Logan, he seems
to have succeeded fairly well in purging himself from his
early fanaticism.

At the time we speak of the friendly circle was unbroken.
It formed a little knot in the weekly meeting of the
Literary Society of the University, in which Bruce read as
an exercise his poem on "The Last Day," and in connection
with which he wrote his "Fable of the Eagle, Crow and
Shepherd."

We have no details or anecdotes of these classic days, no
record of the "Noctes Ambrosianæ." We love to picture
Bruce holding the place among his college companions so
gracefully assigned by Tennyson to the youthful Hallam in
the following lines :—

> " Thy converse drew us with delight
>   The men of rathe and riper years :
>   The feeble soul, a haunt of fears,
> Forgot his weakness in thy sight.
>
> On thee the loyal-hearted hung,
>   The proud was half disarmed of pride,
>   Nor cared the serpent at thy side
> To flicker with his double tongue.

The stern were mild when thou wert by,
The flippant put himself to school
And heard thee,—and the brazen fool
Was softened and he knew not why."

We know that Bruce was an excellent student. Dr
Anderson says, "He applied himself to the several branches
of literature with remarkable assiduity and success. Of the
Latin and Greek languages he acquired a masterly knowledge,
and he made eminent progress in Metaphysics, Mathematics,
and Moral and Natural Philosophy. But the Belles Lettres
was his favourite pursuit, and poetry his darling study."
That one of Bruce's fine, unselfish, genial temperament, with
ready mastery of thought and language, must have made a
charming companion we can easily imagine, and, indeed, we
know from those who came across his path nearer home on
to the close of his brief life. One who was well acquainted
with him, during his short stay at Gairney Bridge, was
wont to say :—"It was like heaven upon earth to be in his
company." Indeed, it is around his life in his native
Kinross that whatever interest there is in his story lies.

The Gairney Bridge school, on the duties of which
Bruce entered at the close of the College session of 1765,
was a very humble beginning in every way. It is clear
there was then no progenitor even of that modern care-
taker, the School Board ; and the poet-teacher was at least
on one occasion driven for solace to the muse, on finding
himself, as he complains, in a "tableless" condition. The old
rickety concern had given way, and there were no means
apparently of finding a substitute. Nor was it an easy
matter to draw in the school fees.

At Gairney Bridge, Michael Bruce met his first and last
Blumine—the Eumelia of "Lochleven."

GAIRNEY BRIDGE AND MONUMENT

"She was," says Dr MacKelvie, "a young woman of modest appearance and agreeable manners, with a large portion of natural good sense. The poet's fancy, however, decked her out with fascinations sufficiently numerous and striking." He believed his love to have been unrequited, and in this strain he refers to it in some of his poems. The young lady was the daughter of the then farmer of Classlochie, and her name was Magdalene Grieve. She was afterwards married to Mr Low of Cleish Mill. She ever fondly cherished the memory of Bruce, but declared that he never told his love. The following stanza, however, native to the soil of Kinross, is sufficiently explicit on the point.

> " In Cleish churchyard lies Magdalene Grieve,
>   A lass o' Bruce the poet,
>   And Tammie Walker made this verse
>   To let the world know it."

At Gairney Bridge,[1] famous as the locality where the fathers of the Secession held their first meeting of Presbytery, Bruce continued to teach for about a year, and was busily engaged during his spare hours, so far as his delicate state of health would permit, in writing poetry, while his friends were urging him to prepare for publication.

[1] See Notes to the Poems, (*h*) p. 207. Near the spot now stands a monument with the following inscription :—

To Commemorate
The Formation of the First Presbytery of the
Secession Church,
At Gairney Bridge, 6th Dec., 1733,
For the maintenance of Scripture Truth, and the Rights
of the Christian People.
Eben. Erskine, Wm. Wilson, Alex. Moncrieff, and Js. Fisher.
Erected. Dec., 1883.

From Gairney Bridge the scene changes to Turfhills, where Bruce resided during his one session at the Kinross Burgher Divinity Hall. The Professor of Theology was Rev. John Swanston of Kinross, much beloved and respected by his students, and almost idolized by his congregation.[1]

Happy in the hospitable abode of the Hendersons of Turfhills, a favourite with his Professor and fellow-students, the time must have passed pleasantly enough in "gay Kinross."

Yet Bruce was all too visibly fading as a leaf, and he was advised by his kind-hearted Professor to give up his studies.

The last summer of the poet's life was partly spent in teaching a school at Forrest Mill, a dreary spot, a few miles from Tillicoultry. He had the misfortune to be thrown from his horse when fording the Devon on his way to this place, and to get so thoroughly drenched that he never fully recovered from the injurious effects. Here he composed his "Lochleven" and the "Elegy: To Spring." In a letter to Mr Arnot he thus philosophizes on the situation : "Things are not very well in this world, but they are pretty well. They might have been worse, and, as they are, may please us who have but a few short days to use them." Writing again to the same friend, he says : "I have written a few lines of a descriptive poem, 'Cui titulus est Lochleven.' You may remember you hinted such a thing to me, so I have set about it, and you may expect a dedication. I hope it will *soon* be finished, as I every week add two lines, blot out six, and alter eight. You shall hear of the plan when I know it myself."[2]

But the young student and teacher was now drawing

[1] Dr Macfarlane's Life of Dr Lawson.
[2] Dr MacKelvie, p. 67.

near the end of the appointed course. He set out one day, on foot, to accomplish the twenty miles of the homeward journey, paying a passing visit to Turfhills on the way. Arrived at his destination, his earthly journeys were now over. He lingered on for some two months in increasing weakness. During this period he was resigned and cheerful. On a friend remarking to him that he was glad to find him so happy, he replied: "And why should not a man be cheerful on the verge of heaven?" "But," said his friend, "you look so emaciated, I am afraid you cannot last long." "You remind me," said the dying youth, "of the story of the Irishman who was told that his hovel was about to fall, and I answer with him: 'Let it fall; it is not mine.'"[1] At last he was found one summer morning, 5th July, 1767, dead in his bed, aged twenty-one years and three months. Beside the sleeper lay his Bible, marked down at Jer. xxii. 10.[2] "Weep ye not for the dead, neither bemoan him"; and on the blank leaf was written:—

> "'Tis folly to rejoice and boast
> How small a price my Bible cost;
> The day of judgment will make clear
> 'Twas very cheap—or very dear."[3]

He was buried in the churchyard of Portmoak. The world was not looking on as the remains of this gifted Christian poet were borne to their last resting-place. But ere long a discovery was made that a true son of song had passed away from the humble abode in Kinnesswood, and since then a train of the noblest of our countrymen has

[1] Letter from daughter of Dr Lawson to Dr MacKelvie.
[2] See Dr MacKelvie, p. 78.
[3] See Notes to the Poems, (*f*) p. 206.

been finding its way to the weaver's cottage in Kinnesswood, and the grave in Portmoak churchyard. The following is the inscription on the monument that marks his resting-place :

To the

Memory of

MICHAEL BRUCE,

Who was born at Kinnesswood in 1746,
And died while a student
In connection with the Secession Church,
In the 21st year of his age.

Meek and gentle in spirit, sincere and unpretending in his Christian deportment, refined in intellect and elevated in character, he was greatly beloved by his friends, and won the esteem of all, while his genius, whose fire neither poverty nor sickness could quench, produced those odes, unrivalled for simplicity and pathos, which have shed an undying lustre on his name.

Early, bright, transient, chaste as morning dew,
He sparkled, and exhaled, and went to heaven.

II.

Writings.

Hos ego versiculos feci tulit alter honores.

— *Virgil.*

II.

WRITINGS.

MICHAEL BRUCE died, as we have seen, before the publication of any of his works. Yet on to the closing scene, and almost to the utmost verge of the valley and shadow through which he was so consciously passing, he continued to pour forth the strains of his swan-like song.

It is clear enough from Bruce's correspondence—in particular from the letters of his fellow-students, Mr Dun and Mr Lawson—that his friends expected him, and that he intended soon, to publish some of his writings. It was the employment of the last months of his life to recast and transcribe into a large quarto volume such of his pieces as he considered fit for the public eye.

There is nothing in the annals of our Scottish literature more pathetic than the history of that quarto volume.

The dying lad's purpose,—no secret to others,—as well as his rare poetic genius, were well known by at least one of his fellow-students at the Edinburgh University, afterwards a minister of the Church of Scotland in Leith—namely, John Logan. Logan, then a young man of nineteen years, was himself an aspirant to literary, and especially poetic, fame. In a certain sense he has achieved both a temporary fame and a permanent notoriety by his connection with Michael Bruce. The story is as follows. A few months after his gentle gifted friend of college days had been laid to rest in Portmoak churchyard, Logan, at that time a tutor in the family of Sir John Sinclair, Bart., visited the poet's father in Kinnesswood. We can imagine him extolling, in courtly phrase, the genius of his former college friend ; and, in short, we know that he so won the fond parent's heart, that the old man was prevailed upon to commit to his trust all his son's MSS. in his possession, including, of course, the large quarto volume, as well as every available scrap of his correspondence, even with Logan himself.

He definitely promised to return the MSS. after the publication of their contents, and assured the father and mother that the proceeds of the published poems of their son would keep them in comfort during the remainder of their lives. Month after month passed, year after year, and no volume of Bruce's appeared, and no explanation from Logan. The anxious, sorrow-stricken father wrote once and again enquiring, but got no reply. At last, after an interval of three years, Logan published a small volume in 1770, entitled, "Poems on several occasions by Michael Bruce." It contained seventeen poems, and a brief laudatory preface to which Logan did not attach his name, though he let it be understood it was from his pen. He gave no memoir of his early friend, not even mentioning the name of his birthplace. Had no other or more friendly hand gathered up the materials for Bruce's touching life-story, we had possessed no record of him. Logan stated that the volume was a miscellany made up of poems "wrote by different authors." He did not, it seems, consider it either necessary or desirable to specify the pieces from the pen of Bruce. Six copies of this little book were sent by the editor to the old folks at Kinnesswood. When the poet's father glanced over it he burst into tears, exclaiming, "Where are my son's 'Gospel Sonnets'?" The allusion is to certain religious poems on which Alexander Bruce, as well as others, knew that Michael had been engaged, at various times, and which he also knew had been committed to Logan when he took in charge the large quarto volume. The phrase "Gospel Sonnets" was familiar, in the Bishop shire, as the designation of the Spiritual Songs of Ralph Erskine, largely composed, it is said, in a wood above his brother's manse in Portmoak. They were, with all their defects, one of the earliest and most successful attempts to advance our Presbyterian hymnology, and then regarded as the "people's classic" in that department. The old man, no doubt, looked forward with pardonable pride to his son's sonnets, one day, taking their place beside those of the other local and honoured poet.

The entire circle of Bruce's friends, in his native place, some of whom had seen Logan's volume before it reached his father, shared in the old man's surprise and disappointment at the absence from its contents, not only of the "Gospel Sonnets," but, indeed, of any pieces, with the exception of the "Elegy : To Spring," indicating the well-known devotional character of the poet's mind.

We will not narrate minutely the incidents of the journey, the first and last, which old Alexander Bruce undertook to the Metropolis to see Logan, and recover the quarto volume of his son's writings and other MSS. He did meet Logan on the street in Leith Walk ; charged him with having kept back the "Gospel Sonnets," and demanded the return of the quarto volume. Logan at first temporized :

C

but in an interview, on the following day, informed his visitor that the quarto volume had gone amissing, and he was afraid "the servants had singed fowls with it." He gave him the MSS. containing a first draught of "The Last Day," "Lochleven," and "Lochleven no More": and with these few scraps of his sacred deposit the broken-hearted father returned to his home under the burden of a new sorrow. From this shock he never fully rallied, and two years after followed his gifted son to the grave.

Not until Logan published his first volume in 1781, entitled, "Poems by the Rev. John Logan, one of the ministers of Leith," was it seen why he had so long delayed, and at length published, in such a peculiar fashion, what he did publish of the "Poems of Michael Bruce." In Logan's volume, the "Ode to the Cuckoo" stood first, and there at last appeared some of the "Gospel Sonnets," the absence of which from the earlier volume had so distressed the poet's father, and so amazed the poet's friends in his native place.

We have, we believe, made it quite clear that Logan acted meanly and falsely in his relations with the poet's family, as regards the MS. volume prepared by Bruce for the press. His dastardly treatment of old Alexander Bruce, when he visited him in Edinburgh, is fitly capped by his ingenious account of the servants singeing the fowls with the large quarto volume. But we have now to face the question—Was Logan capable of going farther, and actually appropriating the authorship of its chief contents?

Logan's volume, published in 1781, contained, as we said, the "Ode to the Cuckoo," which had already appeared in the edition of what he calls "Poems on several occasions by Michael Bruce," and also certain hymns which have, ever since, been claimed by Bruce's friends as being a portion of the "Gospel Sonnets" whose loss had so grieved the father in 1770.

About the same time as Logan published his own Poems, he took out an interdict against the printers and publishers of what is known as the Stirling edition of Bruce's Poems. It was merely a reprint of the miscellany of 1770. Logan claimed to have proprietary rights over this edition, on the ground that Bruce had entrusted to him the publication of his works. Never did he say to his agent, Mr Young, that he was the author of the Cuckoo, during these legal proceedings. Logan was proved to have been guilty of falsehood in stating that Michael Bruce had left his works to his charge. His proprietary rights, in any form, were disallowed, and the Stirling edition was published in 1782. Mr Young, Logan's agent, wrote Dr MacKelvie on the appearance of his Work, expressing his approbation, and recognizing his services—in the justice he had done "to the talents and memory of a most extraordinary youth, more especially by rescuing them from the fangs of a poisonous reptile." [1]

That the "Ode to the Cuckoo" belongs to Bruce, and not to Logan, has been proved to the hilt, by those who have carefully done justice to the evidence. The main points of this manifold testimony are these. The Cuckoo was, from the first, consistently assigned to Bruce by all his friends in Portmoak acquainted with his writings. David Pearson, one of the most intimate and appreciative of all Bruce's friends, on visiting his father, after the poet's death, heard him read the Ode from the quarto volume. Pearson was himself well acquainted with it, and held that the original version was the form in which it appears in the volume of

[1] Grosart, p. 67.

1770. John Birrel, the trusted friend of both father and son, had also heard the father read the poem, and was certain of the Bruce authorship. Professor Davidson, Aberdeen, son of Dr Davidson, Kinross, bore witness that he had seen the poem in what was certified to him to be Bruce's handwriting, with his signature attached, and, underneath, the note in the same handwriting—"You will think I might have been better employed than writing about a Gowk." Dr Baird,[1] who at first ascribed the Ode to Logan, after corresponding with John Birrel, included it in his edition of the poems of Bruce. Dr Baird's conversion to the Bruce authorship, after he had led Dr Anderson to attribute it to Logan in his British Poets, is surely noteworthy. Principal Shairp, in his reply to Dr Laing's brochure on the side of Logan in "Good Words," 1873, justly remarks: "This fact of Principal Baird having changed his mind, after enquiry, is a weighty one, both from the great worth and solidity of his character, and also because his ecclesiastical leanings, if he had listened to them, would have naturally biassed him to side with Logan rather than Bruce." In explanation of Dr Baird's change of mind, Mr Hervey, merchant, Stirling, in a letter to Mr John Birrel, says—"He (Dr Baird) has found the Cuckoo to be Bruce's, and has the original in his own handwriting."[2] Dr Laing's attempt to invalidate the

---

[1] See Appendix B, p. 67.

[2] The circumstances of John Hervey's acquaintance with the Poems of Bruce, and the impression made upon him by reading, for the first time, the Elegy in Spring, are finely related by Dr MacKelvie. The devout and cultured Stirling merchant—looking forward to an early summons into the Great Presence—found, in the Elegy, a power to sustain and cheer him which he had never before experienced from any source— outside the inspired Word itself. This incident led Mr Hervey, along

argument for Bruce goes on the assumption that his
claims are only supported by traditions and recollections:
that in two copies of the Miscellany of 1770 he had seen
Logan's name, "in a contemporary hand," attached to the
"Ode to the Cuckoo"; that Logan had no conceivable
motive for his alleged dishonesty ; and, further, that certain
friends, among the rest a Mrs Hutchison, Logan's cousin,
had actually seen the Ode in his handwriting a short time
before its publication.[1] Now we see no reason, with Dr
Laing, to regard as no proof, even oral traditions or
statements from such men as David Pearson and John
Birrel, on a plain matter of fact. But we have shewn that
their testimony, as well as that of other equally credible
witnesses, does not exist in mere oral tradition, but in
documentary form. It would take all the refined
scepticism of a Hume to invalidate such testimony.
That copies of the Ode, in his own handwriting,
should have been seen by some of his friends before the
publication of the Ode need not surprise us when we know
that Logan had, in his possession, the Bruce MSS. three
years before that date. In fine, there was an only too

with a few Stirling friends, to form the project of bringing out a new
edition of the Poems with what was still a desideratum, a Memoir of
their Author. The purpose was only relinquished when it was understood that the task had been undertaken by Dr Baird. We need hardly
add that any service in his power, in collecting materials for the
Principal's edition, was most cordially rendered.

[1] It ought not to be forgotten in this connection that Lord MacKenzie
bears witness that Logan was in the habit of copying out pieces of poetry
that were not his own composition. He had, he says, seen the "Ode to the
Cuckoo" in what he understood to be Logan's handwriting—but he saw
other pieces copied from well-known authors—and his inference therefore
is, "that he might have written out the Cuckoo, though written
originally by Bruce, as he copied others." See MacKelvie. p. 119.

manifest motive to an unscrupulous literary ambition in the whole conduct of Logan.

We might have referred to other items of evidence. There is abundant material. There is the testimony of Bruce's fellow-students, both at the University and Theological Hall. There is the evidence of Mr Bennet of Gairney Bridge, specially mentioned by Lord Commissioner Adam. There is the fact that many of the villagers could repeat the Ode, from copies furnished by the poet, before its publication. There is the well-remembered comment of Bruce's mother, on the occasion of some one shooting a cuckoo—"Will that be the bird our Michael made a sang about?" There is, however, no need of further witness, so far as external evidence is concerned. Interesting and suggestive as the *internal* evidence is, we shall do little more than barely touch upon it. The diction of the Ode is, we think, far more in keeping with the chaste simplicity of Bruce than the artificial elegance of Logan. The verbal changes of the latter are, in the opinion of a most competent critic, Principal Shairp, none of them happy, and rather betray an alien hand. We might also instance words in the Ode which are favourites of Bruce in his other pieces. But we pass over that peculiarity, noticeable chiefly of course in the original form of the lyric as it appears in the edition of 1770, only noting one of these suggestive indications. We do not know that it has been remarked that the expression "vocal vale" (line 2 verse 5), describing the haunts of Bruce's Cuckoo, is singularly appropriate as corresponding to the local designations for Bruce's surroundings, viz. :—"The *Vale* of Kinross," "The *Vale* of Leven." We add but one other confirmation. It has been proved that Logan wrote, in a copy of the Ode committed to Dr Grant, his executor, after the verse, "Sweet bird," etc., the following stanza, which, however, for some reason, he did not wish him to insert in the edition of his poems.

> " Alas, sweet bird, not so my fate,
>   Dark scowling skies I see
> Fast gathering round and fraught with woe
>   And wintry years to me."

No one will question how strikingly this is in the vein of the author of the "Elegy : To Spring." Principal Shairp regards it as jarring on the *joyous* sentiment of the Ode as a whole. But, a little afterwards, he finely observes : "There is throughout all (the Ode) an undertone of pathetic reference to human sadness, the more impressive that it is only an undertone." There is then nothing strange should that tone be somewhat more distinctly audible in one single verse than in any of the others. It forms, indeed, a link between the foregoing and concluding stanza, and is one of the strongest of the internal indications that the whole is from the hand of Bruce. We see no good reason why this "wandering verse" should not have been inserted by Dr Grant. Dr MacKelvie, for some reason, perhaps because it was not brought under his notice by Mr Miller, does not include it. Dr Grosart, however, giving us the earlier form of the lyric as it appeared in 1770, at the same time inserts the missing stanza, and so clinches the argument from the internal evidence for the Bruce authorship of the entire Ode.

We come now to the important question of Bruce's position as a religious Hymn-writer. When old Alexander Bruce exclaimed, on glancing over the Miscellany in 1770,

"Where are my son's 'Gospel Sonnets'?" he raised a question which was yet to exercise deeply the thoughts of not a few earnest and fair-minded men in generations still to come. It is surely now high time that this pathetic question were answered once for all. We can hardly consider it satisfactory to reply with Dr R. Small in his able article in "The British and Foreign Evangelical Review," 1879, that the Sonnets were wisely consigned by Logan to deserved oblivion. We are pleased to think that they, or some of them, were destined to reappear, and take their proper place in our sanctuary song.

But we must now go back a step in our review, and explain how Bruce came to be known locally as a writer of sacred poetry, and particularly Scripture Paraphrases. About 1764, young Bruce, then only eighteen years of age, joined Mr Buchan's Singing Class in Kinnesswood. At the request of the teacher of the class Bruce replaced some doggerel rhymes, then in use, by composing pieces suited in matter and form to the ideal of a class for sacred music. The members of the class got copies of these compositions, sung them together, and, in many cases, committed them to memory. When Bruce's Poems at length appeared in the village, they took it as a matter of course, that they would contain these characteristic pieces. Hence the amazement and suspicion of foul play when it was discovered that not one of these hymns had a place in the volume. The loss of his son's "Gospel Sonnets" broke the father's heart. The aged saint assuredly cared less about mere literary renown for his son, than a place of honour among those who were to shape into tuneful song the message of the gospel. And now that lingering hope was blighted, and with it also the grand ambition of his life.

Dr Small, in the article to which we have referred, proceeds to solve or rather cut the Gordian knot of the mystery of the disappearance of the "Sonnets," by explaining that Logan destroyed them because he found—he and Dr Robertson—that they were unfit for publication. Logan himself would have sworn that the "servants" were the incendiaries. We must choose between Dr Robertson's statement that Logan destroyed the MSS., and Logan's own declaration that "the servants" were the culprits. It may be both parties had some hand in the transaction. It was in truth no easy matter to burn out the genius of Michael Bruce. Dr Small's allegation that Logan could not find a single "Gospel Sonnet" among the finished works of Bruce, committed to his trust, which came up to "the standard of editorial requirements," is both gratuitous and absurd. He admits that Bruce was a poet of a far higher grade than Logan; and yet thinks it credible that, while Logan could produce so much fitted to adorn our hymnology, not one of the sacred poems of Bruce, in their finished form, could be deemed worthy to see the light. This is his explanation of the fate of Bruce's "Gospel Sonnets." It is also a fair specimen of the style of argument all through his resolute defence of Logan. The hymn controversy cannot be disposed of in this chivalrous fashion even to save the credit of Logan. Nor will it do to amuse us by showing how certain words and phrases are also found in Logan's other pieces, notably in Runnamede. Dr Small admits that Logan did pilfer certain portions of these paraphrases from Bruce, as in the case of the 8th and 18th in the Assembly's collection. Quite competent witnesses have placed it beyond doubt that he pilfered whole paraphrases as well as portions. If Logan could appropriate paraphrases,

or even portions of them, we need not split hairs as to his
snatching of a mere word or phrase. The man who could
take the one unacknowledged from his friend could as easily
take the other. With Bruce's MSS. in his possession,
Logan could very easily, perhaps unconsciously, give
certain phrases in them currency in any poems he might
construct, even in Runnamede itself! We do not think
it is quite clear that he would not have done so even
intentionally had he foreseen that it was likely to serve
the purpose it is meant to do in Dr Small's article. We
quite admit that, as Dr Small states, Dr MacKelvie may
have been mistaken in considering that, say, the 18th
paraphrase was out and out an original production of
Bruce ; and Dr Grosart may have failed to note the
grounds on which four, instead of the one he mentions, of
the poems claimed by him for Bruce were in some degree
revisions of older pieces. This does not, we think, much
affect the general contention, that they bear upon them the
impress of the genius of the finer poet. If these pieces are
revisions, then Logan's dishonesty is proved. Dr Small
says that Logan placed them among the paraphrases
without asserting whether they were or were not entirely
original. But all the five so specified by Dr Small are
found not only in the collection of paraphrases, but also in
Logan's own book. There they are published as avowedly
his, without note or comment ; a claim which, under such
circumstances, is utterly out of court.

Once more, ere we briefly state our case for the Bruce
authorship of the whole list claimed by Dr Grosart, and
ultimately by Dr MacKelvie, we must dispose of a singular
judgment in Dr Small's article, to the effect that it is not
probable that Bruce laboured at the old paraphrases at all.

and that there is no evidence whatever that he did so. We might urge in reply that a wide circle of Bruce's friends, in Portmoak and elsewhere, have even vehemently so testified; but this might not perhaps be regarded as conclusive evidence. We shall therefore fall back upon Dr Small himself. He distinctly states, and proves to his own satisfaction, and that of every reader capable of forming an opinion, that Bruce did write paraphrases. Further, if the stanza, "The beam that shines," etc., which Dr Small admits Bruce wrote, be accepted as from him, he displays great power in that style of composition. In short, Dr Small settles for us the point beyond all dispute, that, however improbable it might seem to him, it is yet a simple fact that Bruce was a religious hymn writer.

The case for Bruce then stands thus. We may divide the hymns and paraphrases in question into two classes, revised and original. In the former class Dr Grosart places hymns 1 and 2 of Logan, corresponding with the 2nd and 18th paraphrases. Dr Small makes out a plausible case for other three, *i.e.*, 23rd, 38th and 59th paraphrases, as belonging also to this class. Yet he admits that in the whole three there are quite original stanzas, and he only "assumes" that the last of the three may be founded on some old paraphrase.

With these explanations in view, we submit the following as a not unfair summary of the grounds on which we have come to the conclusion we have reached as to Bruce's claims. For the authorities which we have consulted we refer the reader to our note on the Bruce-Logan literature in Appendix A, p. 61. Our summary is as follows:—

I.   (1) (Par. viii.)   "Few are thy days and full of woe."
    (2) (Par. xi.)   "O happy is the man who hears."
    (3) (Par. xviii.)   "Behold the mountain of the Lord."

These three, on the superabundant evidence of Dr MacKelvie, who includes them all in his collection, were at once, on the publication of Logan's poems, recognized as belonging to Bruce. The witnesses were personal friends of the poet who were able to quote stanzas of these pieces before they appeared in print.

II. (4) (Par. xxxviii.) " When Jesus by the Virgin brought."
    (5) (Logan, Hymn 3.) "Almighty Father of mankind."
    (6) (Par. xxiii.) " Behold the Ambassador divine."
    (7) Logan, Hymn 12.) "Messiah ! at Thy glad approach."
    (8) (Par. lviii.) " Where high the heavenly temple stands."

These were all claimed by Bruce's friends when Logan's book appeared, *e.g.*, the poet's brother James, and the members of the singing class.

III. (9) (Par. ix.) " Who can resist the Almighty arm?"
    (10) (Par. x.) " In streets and openings of the gate."
    (11) (Par. xxxi.) " Thus speaks the heathen : How shall man."
    (12) (Par. lxiii.) "Take comfort, Christians, when your friends."
    (13) (Hymn 5.) " The hour of my departure's come."

The foregoing is the classification of Mr Julian's Article in his " Dictionary of Hymnology " (1892), in which we have an admirable tabular statement by him (in keeping with the high standard of that work) of the arguments for Bruce and Logan. We accept the classification, but not the conclusion of that Article as regards the last five mentioned paraphrases. While admitting the Bruce claim on the others, the editor of the Hymnology is not clear that the evidence warrants him in assigning these five to Bruce, and so he gives the defendant the benefit of the doubt, and assigns them meantime, till clearer evidence is brought forward, to Logan.

Now, the alleged weakness of the evidence, for these five, lies in the fact, that, as they are not in Logan's book, but only in the Assembly's Paraphrases, Bruce's friends were less prompt to discover them than the other pieces. Yet, whenever Logan's claim (in Cameron's list [1]) directed attention to them, they were at once recognized. Mr Julian suggests that the friends of Bruce in this case argued that as Logan had confessedly stolen so much he must have stolen all. This, of course, might not be very good logic, but Bruce's friends had no need so to reason. Their argument was that they knew the pieces to be his ; and, in addition, it surely was quite fair to hold that, as Logan had stolen a good deal, he might very probably have stolen the whole. Dr Grosart informs us, with graphic detail, and no one can well question the importance of such a testimony, that Dr MacKelvie had expressly promised to furnish him with documentary proof of Bruce's claim. Dr MacKelvie assured him that he had abundant evidence to prove his contention, and said, "Every one of the eleven paraphrases belongs to Bruce—everyone ; and if I ever print the poems again they'll all go in." [2]

In the face of the evidence adduced on the side of Bruce there can, we think, be only one verdict. But even were it otherwise, a clear statement of proof must be made on the other side to justify any claim on the part of Logan. It is not enough for our opponents simply to imagine that

---

[1] Cameron's list. Rev. W. Cameron, Kirknewton. A list assigning the names associated with the pieces in the Scottish Translations and Paraphrases issued by order of the General Assembly in 1781.

[2] See Dr Grosart, p. 102, with Dr Small's reference to what he calls "Dr Grosart's astounding statement" in his Article "Michael Bruce versus John Logan," *British and Foreign Evangelical Review*, 1879, p. 298, footnote.

they have invalidated Bruce's claim. They must establish, on reliable evidence, the claim of Logan. This has not been done, and, we believe, cannot be done.

Nor does Logan's literary or other reputation greatly help them in this task. No one disputes that Logan, apart altogether from his connection with Bruce, has been convicted of acts of gross plagiarism. It has been proved that he, in his no doubt elegant sermons, appropriated Sherlock and Blair, as well as others. When a candidate for one of the Chairs of the Edinburgh University he laid claim to a course of Lectures which were afterwards proved not to be his own. Logan, personally, was just such a man as one might suppose capable of such conduct. His habits of life were so questionable, and his slavery to strong drink so manifest, that he had, for decency's sake, to retire from the ranks of the ministry at a time when the prevailing notions of intemperance were by no means so strict as in our day.

With common fidelity to the claims of friendship, and a diligent use of his own very considerable talents, Logan would have been remembered with esteem and even affection, because of his services on behalf of Michael Bruce. Surely there are few things, in literary story, more tragic than this outcome of what seemed no doubt, to the old folks at Kinnesswood, a warm trustful college friendship, when Logan paid them his fateful visit. We are willing to believe every good thing we possibly can of Bruce's friend : but we cannot forget that, as the gentle, high-souled scholar and poet reeled and fell to the earth, Logan's was the hand that struck what was meant to be a fatal blow to his literary fame. Such was the In Memoriam which was his tribute to early days of converse with one of the finest, truest spirits of our poetic literature.

As to Bruce's other Poems, so far as any controversy is concerned, we have only to say that such comments as may seem to be called for, will be found either in a footnote to such pieces, in introductory notes, or in the concluding appendix. These pieces are taken mostly from the edition of 1770, the few MSS. recovered by Bruce's father, his own correspondence, and family records.

We have now reached the limits we had set ourselves, for consideration, in this form of the Bruce-Logan controversy. The reader, who wishes to go fully into this whole subject, will find that we have done our best to give him what assistance we could in the list of authorities drawn up, and the résumé of the main arguments, with references in detail at the close of this necessarily brief introduction.

It is perhaps not so much the fashion, as it has been, to express pity for those " who have been so ill-advised as to excite an uncalled-for controversy over the grave of the meek Bruce." [1]

The fortunes of the conflict have been suggesting somewhat more temperate modes of speech. Yet the old errors and fallacies are still doing duty in this cause. We are still reminded, even in quarters where we have some right to expect better guidance, that the claim on behalf of Bruce was not made until fifty years after his death, and that Bruce's friends did not, till then, challenge the claims of Logan. We are still asked to believe that Logan's reputation, and Logan's bare assertion, are sufficient evidence of his pretensions.

But these falsities are being exposed ; and in this connection, we refer, with pleasure, to the well-informed, effective article, on this subject, in the "Dictionary of National

[1] See Dublin University Magazine, 1875.

Biography," 1886. We have now done with the din of controversy. In what follows we shall endeavour to give some estimate of the works of Bruce, and their promise of future excellence, had their author lived, as in the case of his English contemporary, Cowper, to give us his mature productions.

The pieces by which we are, for the most part, able to form a judgment on the rank of Bruce as a poet, are only a few first efforts, so far as they have escaped destruction, whose native simplicity is more or less unimpaired by the garish embellishments of Logan. Further, these pieces were written under every conceivable disadvantage, both as to their author's health and circumstances. It would be no more fair to estimate Bruce's possible greatness by this volume of poems, than it would be to form our estimate of Henry Kirke White from the " Remains " we have of him, or of Byron from an examination of his "Hours of Idleness." When we remember, as we glance over the poems, that Bruce died when he had little more than completed his twenty-first year, we cannot fail to be impressed by the rare quality of his mind, its freedom from puerilities and pomposities which often, even in the best intellects, as in the case of such a man as the Poet of the "Seasons," only yield slowly to a finer temper. There is an exquisite finish about all that Bruce had really time to give his strength to, and it comes out especially in his shorter pieces, the "Ode to the Cuckoo," and "Hymns and Paraphrases." "Lochleven," and the "Last Day," his longest poems, contain passages of great power, but neither piece is finished as the artist could have done, had he been spared to do his best. The poetical writings of Bruce embrace specimens of the lyric, the elegy, the satire, the ballad, the sustained descriptive style, as well as of distinctively religious composition. This alone vouches for the adaptability of his powers. Johnson, in substance, defines genius as a naturally powerful mind whose faculties are accidentally concentrated on some absorbing subject of interest. Bruce is always masterly, whether grave or gay, and he is both the one and the other.

In the Ode to the Cuckoo he is considered to be at his best. Edmund Burke regarded it as the most beautiful Lyric in the English tongue. The language is natural, choice, emotional. The whole is in striking contrast to the artificial style and diction of the age. The theme itself is happily chosen, embodying, as Principal Shairp says, "all that is most delightful in the childhood of life and the year."

The bird-world is ever a region of inspiration, to the poet of nature. Its airy inhabitants are winged messengers from the skies, each with its angelic voice of sympathy with man in joy or sorrow. It is as if the Great Spirit moved in them, and sent by them, and by each of them, some mystic token of the all-wise, all-loving heart, which throbs throughout the pulses of existence. Some of the noblest lyrics that grace our literature, we owe to this subtle, soul-inspiring influence. It has given us "The Ode to a Skylark" of Shelley ; the ode "To the Cuckoo" of Wordsworth : and Hogg's "Bird of the Wilderness, blithesome and cumberless."

More recently William Watson in one of his most finished productions, "The first Skylark of Spring," shews us the same potent influence as it appeals to the imagination of our younger poets.

Here is how, in a single verse, he describes the sweet singer and its mission to man :—

D

" For thou art native to the spheres,
  And of the courts of heaven art free,
  And carriest to his temporal ears,
  News from eternity."

The Ode to the Cuckoo is conceived in this spirit.
Every verse in it bespeaks the *curiosa felicitas* of thought
and language which is the endowment of the true poet.
The sixth verse is peculiarly happy, as fitly interpreting
the message of the bird of Spring.

Sweet bird ! thy bower is ever green,
  Thy sky is ever clear ;
  Thou hast no sorrow in thy song,
  No winter in thy year.

The lines linger on the ear, and engrave themselves upon
the heart as with a diamond.

We pass from the Ode to note Bruce's next department
of literary work—the Hymns and Paraphrases. The circumstances which led Bruce into this species of composition
have already been related.

The cause of sacred Hymnology was slowly moving
forward in Scotland somewhat before Bruce's day. The
Hymns and Spiritual Songs of Dr Watts had originated a
new movement in England, and this movement had been
further advanced by Dr Doddridge, the author, among
other hymns, of the second paraphrase, " O God of Bethel."
It was still further promoted when it enlisted on its
side the saintly genius of Cowper and the talent of John
Newton, in the Olney Hymns. Slowly but surely the
wave of grave sweet melody broke over the heart of
Scotland. Ralph Erskine was one of the first to take up
and locate the strain. His "Gospel Sonnets" were, in their

day, the people's classic. These were written in a quaint
style, and sometimes were dryly doctrinal. But Erskine
was, none the less, a true "Makkar," and capable, when
he did himself justice, of reaching a high level of poetic
excellence.

In the Scottish Establishment Hymns and Paraphrases
were being introduced into family and church worship.
Bruce, as we have seen, was led to take some share in this,
no doubt to him, congenial service. These Hymns and
Paraphrases were his father's favourite pieces. They are
the productions of Bruce's muse, with which we are all
best acquainted. They are well known beyond the bounds
of Scotland and England. Their lines and stanzas are
household words wherever the Presbyterian form of worship
is observed, and far beyond its pale.

We reckon Bruce's Hymns and Paraphrases among the
choicest compositions of their kind in our language. They
can well stand comparison with similar efforts. Dr Watts,
with all his gifts and graces, is supposed at times to get
somewhat commonplace in his Hymns, although he every
now and again reminds his reader that he belongs to a high
order of poets. Nowhere has there been more frequent
and disastrous failure than in this kind of composition.
Cowper, who was certainly a competent judge of the
matter, plaintively sings :—

> " Pity religion has so seldom found
> A skilful guide into poetic ground."

The Olney poet was himself one of those skilful guides ; and
it lay in Michael Bruce, had he been spared to give us the
mature productions of his genius, to have taken his place
beside him.

We will not enter into any analysis of the Bruce Paraphrases. We consider Paraphrase eighth, as he originally wrote it, and not as cut down for insertion in the Paraphrases for public worship, as one of the finest strains of the poet in the serious vein. " Who can resist " is a piece of singular sublimity ; and there is a noble treatment of a great theme in the fifty-eighth, " Where high the heavenly temple stands."

In all this criticism it is remembered that we rather trace indications, than estimate finished work. But, with this obvious proviso, we place Bruce's " Gospel Sonnets " in the front rank of their class.

We had purposed to say something on the " Elegy : To Spring," and on " Lochleven." But we can only refer to them and the miscellaneous pieces in a few sentences. Bruce's Elegy is perhaps the most touching of all his writings. It has borne the healing balm to many a wounded spirit. Lord Craig fixes upon it as the gem of the edition of 1770. It has been said there is only one other Elegy in the English language to compare with the " Elegy : To Spring." If we can place it side by side with Gray's masterpiece, let us not forget that while Gray laboured for seven years, in the midst of every literary help, to perfect the earlier Elegy, Bruce began and completed his task during the few months of sickly toil at Forrest Mill, with no resources save his own unaided genius. Nor can we forget that while the Cambridge poet's song, sweet as it is in expression, is after all a song of everlasting night, the other is inspired by the glory of the coming day. Compare or rather contrast the sentiment of the well-known lines :—

" Beneath these rugged elms, that yew tree's shade,
  Where heaves the turf in many a mouldering heap,
Each in his narrow cell for ever laid,
  The rude forefathers of the hamlet sleep."

with the last stanza of Bruce's Elegy :—

" There let me sleep forgotten in the clay,
  When death shall shut these weary aching eyes :
Rest in the hope of an eternal day
  Till the long night's gone and the last morn arise."

It would take long to point out either the merits or defects of Bruce's "Lochleven." There is the curious absence, in the poem, of any reference to Mary's imprisonment in the castle. There is the episode of the love story of Levina to which, in its bearing upon the Bruce–Logan controversy, we have referred elsewhere. Few will deny its more than romantic charm. The discovery of Levina, reminding us of that of another Lady of the Lake, is thus described :—

" Her, as she halted on a green hill-top,
A quiver'd hunter spied. Her flowing locks.
In golden ringlets glitt'ring to the sun,
Upon her bosom play'd : her mantle green,
Like thine, O Nature ! to her rosy cheek
Lent beauty new ; as from the verdant leaf
The rose-bud blushes with a deeper bloom,
Amid the walks of May."

The story ends, as we might have supposed, in plunging or merging the "Naiad of the Vale" into the Lake "which yet retains her name." This, we may after all presume, was her native element. There we can imagine her coming to herself again, and developing even greater charms than of yore. Nor need we doubt that she will reappear, to enact her world-old drama, when another

Bruce shall arise to call her up by his potent enchantments. But the piece is striking mainly from its descriptive power, its photograph not only of Lochleven, but largely also of the Vale of Kinross. Composed in haste, under the incubus of failing health, it is an evidence of what the writer could have achieved under other circumstances.

As to the Miscellaneous Pieces, we have only left ourselves space to say that they abound in airy flights of the muse, and in rich humour little akin, some might imagine, to the serious cast of Bruce's mind. Yet humour, if true, is only the other side of a deeply serious nature which sees the too often grim and sad reality, and also, side by side, its ridiculous parody. In any case, Bruce could be gay when the mood came upon him ; as witness such pieces as, "Anacreontic: To a Wasp," or "The Musiad: A Minor Epic Poem." Here is how he describes the death of the Mouse.

> " The farmer lifts his armed hand,
>   And on the mouse inflicts an wound.
> What mouse could such a blow withstand ?
>   He fell, and, dying, bit the ground.
> Thus Lambris fell, who flourished long
>   (I half forgot to tell his name),
> But his renown lives in the song,
>   And future times shall speak his fame."

We might instance several other pieces in this style, such as the "Fall of the Table," enclosed in a letter to Mr Flockhart of Annafrech, who was manager of Bruce's Gairney Bridge School. The same sportive vein can be traced in what we have of Bruce's writings in the form of letters to his friends. One piece—"A Dialogue" on his school experiences—gives at once some insight into the poet's circumstances, and his invincible sprightliness of spirit. The Dialogue is as follows.

"As I was about to enter on my labours for the week. an old fellow like a Quaker came up and addressed me thus :—

"Q. Peace be with you, friend.

"M. Be you also safe.

"Q. I have brought my son Tobias to thee, that thou mayest instruct him in the way that he should go.

"M. He is welcome.

"Q. Our brother Jacob telleth me that thou shewest thyself a faithful workman, hearing thy scholars oftener in a day than others, because thou hast few.

"M. I presume I do.

"Q. Verily, therein thou doest well : thou shalt not lose thy reward : it shall be given thee with the faithful in their day.

"M. Ay, but, friend, I need somewhat in present possession.

"Q. I understand you : thou wouldst have the prayers of the faithful.

"M. Ay, and something more substantial ; in short, I must have two shillings per quarter for teaching your son Tobias.

"Q. Ah! friend, I perceive thou lovest the mammon of unrighteousness : let me convince you of your sin.

"M. Certainly, since thou seemest to be a most righteous man, who deemeth the servant worthy of his hire.

"Q. Hearken unto my voice : Ezekiel, who was also called Holdfast, took but sixpence in the quarter, as thou callest it. He was a good man, but he sleepeth ; the faithful mourned for him. He catechised the children seven times a day. He was one of the righteous, yea, he was upright in his day save in the matter of ——.

"M. I still think that the labour you expect me to bestow on your son Tobias is worth two shillings a quarter.

"Q. Two shillings! verily, friend, thou art an extortioner: yea, thou grindest the face of the poor: yea, thou lovest filthy lucre. Thou hast respect unto this present world. *Cætera desunt.*"

Bruce, however, will be remembered and loved rather as a master of grave, sweet melody, than as a humorist either in prose or verse. His mind was characteristically devotional, and it was as a religious poet that he was regarded and admired in his own native village before his name was heard outside its narrow precincts.

No one can peruse the writings of Bruce without being touched by their thrilling pathos, befitting, as Carlyle would say, an earnest man ever looking into the dark continent of death and eternity. Here is how he writes to his friend Pearson, in view of his approaching end, somewhat in the strain of Addison's "Vision of Mirza."

> " If morning dreams presage approaching fate,
>   And morning dreams, as poets tell, are true,
> Led by pale ghosts I enter death's dark gate,
>   And bid this life and all the world adieu."

"A few mornings ago as I was taking a walk on an eminence which commands a view of the Forth, with the vessels sailing along, I sat down, and taking out my Latin Bible, opened by accident at a place in The Book of Job ix. 23—'Now my days are passed away as the swift ships.' Shutting the book, I fell a-musing on this affecting comparison. Whether the following happened to me in a dream or waking reverie I cannot tell: but I fancied myself on the bank of a river or sea, the opposite side of which was hid from view, being involved in clouds of mist. On the shore stood a multitude, which no man could number, waiting for passage. I saw a great many ships taking in passengers, and several persons going about in the garb of pilots, offering their service. Being ignorant, and curious to know what all these things meant, I applied to a grave old man who stood by, giving instructions to the departing passengers. His name, I remember, was the Genius of human life.

"'My son,' said he, 'you stand on the banks of the stream of Time. All these people are bound for Eternity, that "undiscovered country from whence no traveller ever returns." The country is very large and divided into two parts; the one is called the Land of Glory, the other the Kingdom of Darkness. The names of those in the garb of pilots are Religion, Virtue, Pleasure. They who are so wise as to choose Religion for their guide have a safe though frequently a rough passage; they are at last landed in the happy climes where sighing and sorrow for ever flee away. They have likewise a secondary director, Virtue. but there is a spurious virtue who pretends to govern by himself; but the wretches who trust in him as well as those who have Pleasure for their pilot are either ship-wrecked or cast away in the Kingdom of Darkness. But the vessel in which you must embark approaches; you must be gone. Remember what depends upon your conduct.' No sooner had he left me than I found myself surrounded by those pilots I mentioned before. Immedi-ately I forgot all that the old man said to me. and seduced by the fair promises of Pleasure, chose him for my director. We weighed anchor with a fair gale; the sky serene, the sea calm. Innumerable little isles lifted their green heads around us covered with trees in full blossom; dissolved in stupid mirth, we were carried on, regardless of the past, of the future unmindful. On a sudden the sky was darkened, the winds roared, the sea raged; red rose the sand from the bottom of the troubled deep. The angel of the waters lifted up his voice. At that instant a strong ship passed by. I saw Religion at the helm. 'Come out from among these,' he cried. I and a few others threw ourselves out into his ship. The wretches were left now tossed on the swelling deep. The waters on every side poured through the riven vessel. They cursed the Lord; when lo! a fiend rose from the deep, and in a voice, like distant thunder, thus spoke: 'I am Abaddon, the first-born of death: ye are my prey; open thou, abyss, to receive them.' As he thus spoke they sank, and the waves closed over their heads. The storm was turned into a calm, and we heard a voice saying, 'Fear not, I am with you. When you pass through the waters they shall not overflow you.' Our hearts were filled with joy. I was engaged in discourse with one of my new companions when one from the top cried out, 'Courage, my friends, I see the fair haven, the land that is yet afar off.' Looking up, I found it was a certain friend who had mounted up for the benefit of contemplating the country before him. Upon seeing *you* I was so affected that I started and awaked. Farewell, my friend, farewell."

We might multiply selections in this strain, but must content ourselves with the concluding stanzas from the "Elegy."

" Now Spring returns : but not to me returns
    The vernal joys my better years have known ;
Dim in my breast life's dying taper burns,
    And all the joys of life with health are flown.

Starting and shivering in the inconstant wind,
    Meagre and pale, the ghost of what I was,
Beneath some blasted tree I lie reclined,
    And count the silent moments as they pass :

The winged moments, whose unstaying speed
    No art can stop, or in their course arrest ;
Whose flight shall shortly count me with the dead.
    And lay me down in peace with them that rest.

Oft morning dreams presage approaching fate ;
    And morning dreams, as poets tell, are true.
Led by pale ghosts, I enter death's dark gate,
    And bid the realms of light and life adieu.

I hear the helpless wail, the shriek of wo ;
    I see the muddy wave, the dreary shore,
The sluggish streams that slowly creep below,
    Which mortals visit, and return no more.

Farewell, ye blooming fields ! ye cheerful plains !
    Enough for me the churchyard's lonely mound,
Where Melancholy with sad Silence reigns,
    And the rank grass waves o'er the cheerless ground.

There let me wander at the shut of eve,
    When sleep sits dewy on the labourer's eyes,
The world and all its busy follies leave,
    And talk with Wisdom where my Daphnis lies.

There let me sleep forgotten in the clay,
    When death shall shut these weary aching eyes,
Rest in the hopes of an eternal day,
    Till the long night 's gone, and the last morn arise."

Thus much for our estimate of Bruce's literary labours, so nobly essayed, so prematurely closed. Never was a finer, purer spirit devoted to the muses. Nor, brief as was his period of personal service, can we for a moment doubt that he successfully accomplished his life-work. We cannot and we need not dissociate, in this case, the man from his writings. That noble nature gives form and power to all that he said and sung.

Burns tells us that the poetic genius of his country found him, as the prophetic bard Elijah did Elisha, at the plough, threw her mantle over him, and he tuned his artless lays as she inspired. The same mysterious visitant, passing by many a goodly mansion in the Vale of Kinross, dropped her mantle upon one of the inmates of a humble cottage in Kinnesswood. We see him as he wraps it around his youthful yet sickly form. We see him as, in due time, he steps forth on his God-given mission. We mark how lovingly, how unweariedly and with what abiding success, that mission is fulfilled.

As long as youthful piety and genius are revered, as long as the voice of hymns and spiritual songs arises from the sanctury gathering, in this and in other lands, so long shall men continue to honour the memory and the muse of Michael Bruce.

APPENDIX A.

I. THE following is a list, in chronological order, of the chief authorities on Bruce's poems and the Bruce-Logan literature referred to in the foregoing pages :—

1. Poems on Several Occasions. By Michael Bruce. Edinburgh, 1770. (Edited by John Logan.)

2. Reflections on genius unnoticed and unknown ; Anecdotes of Michael Bruce. Lord Craig. (Article in " Mirror," Edinburgh, 1779.)

3. Poems. By the Rev. Mr Logan, one of the ministers of Leith. London, 1781.

4. Poems on Several Occasions by Michael Bruce. Stirling, 1782.

5. Lives of the British Poets. Dr Anderson. 1795.

6. Poems on Several Occasions. By Michael Bruce. Edinburgh, 1796. (Edited by Dr Baird.)

7. Poems and Runnamede. A Tragedy. By the Rev. John Logan, F.R.S., one of the ministers of Leith. Edinburgh, 1812.

8. Poetical Works of Michael Bruce and John Logan. By Thomas Park. London, Stanhope Press, 1813.

9. Life and Poems of Bruce. Dr MacKelvie. Edinburgh, 1837.

10. Works of Michael Bruce. Dr Grosart. Edinburgh, 1865.

11. Ode to the Cuckoo. David Laing. Edinburgh, 1873. (Pamphlet).

12. Michael Bruce and the Ode to the Cuckoo. Principal Shairp. "Good Words," 1873.

13. The Encyclopædia Britannica. Ninth Edition. Edinburgh, Adam and Charles Black, 1876.

14. Michael Bruce and Authorship of the Ode to the Cuckoo. Dr John Small. "British and Foreign Evangelical Review," 1877.

15. Michael Bruce *versus* John Logan. Rev. Dr R. Small. "British and Foreign Evangelical Review," 1879.

16. Dictionary of National Biography. London, 1886.

17. Dictionary of Hymnology. Julian. London, 1892.

II. In order that the reader may more easily satisfy himself as to the validity of the main arguments adduced for the Bruce authorship of the "Ode to the Cuckoo" and "Hymns and Paraphrases," we subjoin the following references in detail.

ODE TO THE CUCKOO.

1. Ode familiar to the villagers of Kinnesswood previous to its publication by Logan, in 1770. Dr MacKelvie, pp. 117, 118 ; also Dr Grosart, pp. 68-72.

Here the chief witnesses are the father, David Pearson, and John Birrel. Pearson was for some time Bruce's room-mate. Both were most intimate friends of the poet, of like literary tastes, and far above all suspicion in regard to their evidence. They were not only able to testify that Bruce was the author of the Ode, but they had both heard it read, or read it for themselves in Bruce's quarto volume. "When I came to visit his father," writes

Pearson to Dr Anderson, "a few days after Michael's death, he went and brought forth his poem book, and read the 'Ode to the Cuckoo' and the 'Musiad,' at which the good old man was greatly overcome." To the same correspondent he writes—"The Cuckoo and the Hymns in the end of Logan's book are assuredly Bruce's productions." Kinnesswood, Aug. 29th, 1795.

2. Ode in the handwriting of Michael Bruce, in possession of Mr Bickerton, Kinnesswood, seen by Professor Davidson. with the note attached, in same handwriting, "You will think I might have been better employed than writing about a Gowk." Dr MacKelvie, pp. 114, 115. The poem was written on a very small quarto page, and Dr MacKelvie suggestively adds, "All Bruce's letters. which we have seen, are written upon half a sheet of long paper, such as boys use for writing copies doubled, which makes a small quarto page."

3. Every argument that could be adduced for Logan's rights was before the Lord Ordinary in 1782. He entirely disallowed even Logan's proprietary rights in the edition of 1770, to say nothing of rights of authorship. Dr MacKelvie, pp. 127-142. Deliberate falsehoods were proved to have been advanced in support of the claim. Logan's own agent in the trial, Alex. Young, W.S., Edinburgh, who must necessarily have been perfectly familiar with all the facts, in a letter to Dr MacKelvie, on the appearance of his book, thus wrote :—"I am really at a loss to express to you my approbation of the manner in which you have executed the work, and the justice you have done to the talents and memory of a most extraordinary youth, more especially by rescuing them from the fangs of a poisonous reptile."

4. Dr Baird, at first, attributes the Ode to Logan, but, after correspondence with Birrel, changes his mind and includes it *not as subsequently altered by Logan, but in its original form*, in his edition of Bruce's Poems. Dr MacKelvie, pp. 116, 117, also "Michael Bruce and 'Ode to the Cuckoo,'" by Principal Shairp. "Good Words," 1873, p. 797. In this finely appreciative article, on the side of Bruce, Principal Shairp mentions, in this connection, the remarkable fact of a similar change of view on the part of Mr John Bright, a few years before his visit to the poet's birth-place in Kinnesswood. "At that time Mr Bright himself believed, as so many others have done, and as some still do, that the Ode was Logan's. Further enquiries convinced him that in this belief he was mistaken, and that Bruce was its real author."

5. Constant oral tradition of villagers of Kinnesswood, corroborated by documentary evidence. "Good Words," 1873, p. 798 ; also letters previously referred to, and others.

6. The testimony of Bruce's fellow-students at the University and Theological Hall. Dr Grosart, p. 77. The evidence of one of these fellow-students is thus referred to by Lord-Chief Commissioner Adam (Dr MacKelvie, pp. 112, 113):—"I ought to have mentioned that Mr Bennet of Gairney Bridge, the seceding clergyman, told me that he believed or *rather that he knew* that Bruce was the author of the Cuckoo."

7. We shall only further refer to the well remembered remark of the poet's mother on a cuckoo being shot near the village, "Will that be the bird our Michael made a sang about ? " (Dr MacKelvie, p. 112), the fact that Bruce was in the habit of furnishing copies of his poems, in his handwriting, to his friends (Dr Grosart, p. 78 ; also,

"Good Words," 1873, p. 797), and finally the circumstance that a copy of the Ode existed among the Baird MSS. "He (*i.e.*, Dr Baird) has found the Cuckoo to be Michael Bruce's, and has the original in his own handwriting."— Letter from Mr Hervey to Mr Birrel. For the bearing of the *internal* evidence on the authorship of the Ode, we refer the reader to Writings, p. 38.

HYMNS AND PARAPHRASES.

1. Circumstances which first led Bruce to write hymns.

From time of Buchan's Singing Class, a new era begins for sacred music in Portmoak.

The "old eight" tunes (*i.e.*, French, Dundee, York, Newton, Elgin, London, Martyrs, Abbey) were enlarged by addition of new ones, and doggerel rhymes replaced by verses composed by Bruce at Buchan's request. See Dr MacKelvie's evidence as to three of these pieces, pp. 102-104.

2. The exclamation of the poet's father, when he first glanced over the Miscellany of 1770, "Where are my son's 'Gospel Sonnets'?" Dr MacKelvie, p. 99.

3. Father, on visiting Logan, demands an explanation of the absence from the volume of his son's "Gospel Sonnets," and learns from him that the quarto volume has been destroyed. Dr MacKelvie, p. 109.

4. The members of the singing class, Kinnesswood, and other villagers, share the father's surprise and disappointment at the absence from the edition of 1770 of any pieces (with the exception of the Elegy) indicating the well known devotional character of Bruce's mind, as well as of the hymns familiar to them, and verses of which they could repeat. Dr MacKelvie, pp. 98, 99.

E

5. Admitted by his biographer, when advocating Logan's claim, that Bruce might have left hymns in a more or less polished state, and these hymns might have been altered, embellished, and published by Logan. Life of Logan prefixed to his Poems, 1812, pp. 20, 21.

6. Villagers of Kinnesswood recognize the lost hymns, or some of them, in Logan's book, 1781. Dr Grosart, p. 92.

7. David Pearson, himself a writer of Paraphrases, and a member of the singing class, says, in a letter to Dr Anderson, "They may as well ascribe to Logan the framing of the Universe as the writing of these Poems." Dr MacKelvie, pp. 105, 106.

8. Evidence of the poet's brother James, "that all the Paraphrases published in Logan's name were written by his brother, and that he had often read them, heard them often repeated, and frequently sung portions of them in Buchan's class long before the Assembly's Collection was heard of." This evidence corroborated by Birrel, who succeeded Buchan as teacher of the singing class. Dr MacKelvie, pp. 104, 105.

9. Dr Grosart's important testimony as to written copies in possession of Dr MacKelvie, since the publication of his first edition, and his emphatic statement to Dr Grosart shortly before his death — "Every one of the eleven Paraphrases belongs to Bruce—every one ; and if ever I print the Poems again, they'll all go in." Dr Grosart, p. 102. Footnote.

APPENDIX B.

DR BAIRD's edition of Bruce's Poems (Edinburgh, 1796) was not merely a reprint but an enlargement of Logan's edition of 1770. The Stirling or second edition of 1782 was such a reprint. But Dr Baird gives us, over and above Logan's Preface (1770), a prefatory note from himself, and Lord Craig's Article in the *Mirror* (1779). There is further added, and as a part of the general introduction or preface, "Verses addressed to the mother of Michael Bruce. By a Lady." It is much to be regretted that the kind-hearted editor did not rather give us, by way of introduction, from the materials in his possession, a sketch of the poet from his own hand. In Dr Baird's book we have the following pieces, from the pen of Bruce, which did not appear in the original Miscellany. "They were taken," says Dr Baird, "from the manuscripts of the Author furnished by his mother." They are :—The Last Day : A Poem   Philocles : An Elegy on the Death of Mr William Dryburgh. The Vanity of our Desire of Immortality here : A Story in the Eastern Manner. But Dr Baird's edition is still further interesting from its connection with the name of Robert Burns. The Ayrshire poet was then a foremost figure in the literary world. His poems had been, when Dr Baird wrote him on this subject (1791), five years before the public.

In such circumstances, Dr Baird bethought him of securing from Burns some pieces which might be included in his forthcoming edition of Bruce.

He wrote him accordingly, stating that the whole profits of the book were to be given to Bruce's "mother, a woman of eighty years of age, poor, and helpless." It is also added that some friends wished to place a humble stone over Bruce's grave, and Burns is requested to furnish the inscription.

The pieces promised by Burns did not ultimately appear, for reasons which we do not consider it necessary to state here ; and he himself passed away from the scene in the year of the publication of Dr Baird's volume. The answer, however, to the Principal's request, is so characteristic of the writer, that it has often been quoted as evidence of the fine qualities of his heart, and may be quoted once more.

It is as follows :—

"Why did you, my dear sir, write to me in such a hesitating style on the business of poor Bruce ? Don't I know, and have I not felt, the many ills that poetic flesh is heir to ? You shall have your choice of all the unpublished poems I have ; and had your letter had my direction, so as to have reached me sooner (it only came to my hand this moment), I should have directly put you out of suspense upon the subject.

"I only ask that some prefatory advertisement in the books, as well as the subscription bills, may bear that the publication is solely for the benefit of the mother.

"I would not put it in the power of ignorance to surmise, or rather to insinuate, that I clubbed a share of the merit from mercenary motives. Nor need you give me credit for any remarkable generosity in my part of the business.

"I have such a host of peccadilloes, failings, follies, and backslidings (anybody but myself would, perhaps, give them a worse appellation) that by way of some balance, however trifling, in the account, I am fain to do any good that occurs in my very limited power to a fellow-creature, just from the selfish purpose of clearing a little the vista of retrospection."

I.

Lochleven

and

The Last Day.

LOCHLEVEN.

LOCHLEVEN.[1]

A POEM.

Lochleven, the subject of Bruce's longest poem, lies towards the east end of the vale of Kinross. To the south and east runs the ridge of the Lomonds. The traces of the landslip on the sides of Benarty give an abrupt and rugged appearance to the southern setting. Further eastward and northward rise the "rocky Lomonds," on whose verdant slopes the young poet first revelled in the quiet beauty of the panorama, of which he was afterwards so nobly to essay the description.

It is now well-nigh 130 years since Bruce laid the scene of his most elaborate descriptive poem, with true poetic instinct, in his own native vale, with its embosomed lake, so replete with stirring memories, both ancient and modern. Since that time, while the main features of this classic region have remained the same, both the aspect of the loch and its surroundings have changed. The castle on its island is here, as of old, with its square tower and rampart, its memories of great political movements, of distinguished inmates, especially of Mary Stuart. St. Serf's has still the ruins of its ancient priory, the traces of its monastery, and its Culdee burying-ground. But even these islands have grown in size since Bruce looked down upon them from the slopes of Bishop Hill, and other smaller islets have lifted up their heads.

By the drainage of the loch in 1830, its area was reduced from 4638 imperial acres to somewhat over 3000; thus exposing, in and around it, a new margin of soil, on which, here and there, adding a fresh charm to the scene, are groves of spruce and pine planted by the Laird of Lochleven.

We do not speak here of the unique interest which belongs to Lochleven from the angler's point of view, except simply to remark that Lochleven trout are everywhere famous for their excellent flavour and bright colour, derived, it is said, from a fresh water mussel on which they

[1] See Life, p. 26. See Writings, p. 53.

feed. We have said enough, we trust, to make it clear that in historical and literary interest of every description, from Wyntoun's "Cronykil of Scotland" on to Bruce's Poems, and Sir Walter Scott's "Abbot," Lochleven may well claim a foremost place among Scottish lakes, and may well have its own native poet.

HAIL, native land! where on the flowery banks
Of Leven Beauty ever-blooming dwells;
A wreath of roses, dropping with the dews
Of Morning, circles her ambrosial locks
Loose-waving o'er her shoulders; where she treads,
Attendant on her steps, the blushing Spring
And Summer wait, to raise the various flow'rs
Beneath her footsteps; while the cheerful birds
Carol their joy, and hail her as she comes,
Inspiring vernal love and vernal joy.

Attend, Agricola![1] who to the noise
Of public life preferr'st the calmer scenes
Of solitude, and sweet domestic bliss,
Joys all thine own! attend thy poet's strain,
Who triumphs in thy friendship, while he paints
The past'ral mountains, the poetic streams,
Where raptur'd Contemplation leads thy walk,
While silent Evening on the plain descends.

Between two mountains, whose o'erwhelming tops,
In their swift course, arrest the bellying clouds,
A pleasant valley lies. Upon the south,
A narrow op'ning parts the craggy hills,
Thro' which the lake, that beautifies the vale,
Pours out its ample waters. Spreading on,

---

[1] Agricola. Mr David Arnot, Proprietor of Portmoak. It was at Arnot's suggestion that Bruce wrote Lochleven. See Life, p. 26.

And wid'ning by degrees, it stretches north
To the high Ochil, from whose snowy top
The streams that feed the lake flow thund'ring down.

The twilight trembles o'er the misty hills,
Trinkling with dews; and whilst the bird of day
Tunes his ethereal note, and wakes the wood,
Bright from the crimson curtains of the morn,
The sun appearing in his glory, throws
New robes of beauty over heav'n and earth.

O now, while nature smiles in all her works,
Oft let me trace thy cowslip-cover'd banks,
O Leven! and the landscape measure round.
From gay Kinross, whose stately tufted groves
Nod o'er the lake, transported let mine eye
Wander o'er all the various chequer'd scene,
Of wilds, and fertile fields, and glitt'ring streams,
To ruin'd Arnot;[1] or ascend the height
Of rocky Lomond, where a riv'let pure
Bursts from the ground, and through the crumbled crags
Tinkles amusive. From the mountain's top,
Around me spread, I see the goodly scene!
Inclosures green, that promise to the swain
The future harvest; many-colour'd meads;
Irriguous vales, where cattle low, and sheep
That whiten half the hills; sweet rural farms
Oft interspers'd, the seats of past'ral love
And innocence; with many a spiry dome
Sacred to heav'n, around whose hallow'd walls
Our fathers slumber in the narrow house.

[1] Ruined Arnot. Arnot Tower, two miles east of Scotland Well.

Gay, beauteous villas, bosom'd in the woods,
Like constellations in the starry sky,
Complete the scene. The vales, the vocal hills,
The woods, the waters, and the heart of man,
Send out a gen'ral song; 'tis beauty all
To poet's eye, and music to his ear.[1]

Nor is the shepherd silent on his hill,
His flocks around; nor schoolboys, as they creep,
Slow-pac'd, tow'rds school; intent, with oaten pipe
They wake by turns wild music on the way.

Behold the man of sorrows hail the light!
New risen from the bed of pain, where late,
Toss'd to and fro upon a couch of thorns,[2]
He wak'd the long dark night, and wish'd for morn.
Soon as he feels the quick'ning beam of heav'n,
And balmy breath of May, among the fields
And flow'rs he takes his morning walk: his heart
Beats with new life; his eye is bright and blithe;
Health strews her roses o'er his cheek; renew'd
In youth and beauty, his unbidden tongue
Pours native harmony, and sings to Heav'n.

In ancient times, as ancient Bards have sung,
This was a forest. Here the mountain-oak
Hung o'er the craggy cliff, while from its top

---

[1] Akenside's Pleasures of Imagination,

> "Thou makest all nature beauty to his eye
> Or music to his ear.

[2] Gray's Ode to Vicissitude,

> "See the wretch that long has tost
> On the thorny bed of pain," &c.

Lochleven.

The eagle mark'd his prey ; the stately ash
Rear'd high his nervous stature, while below
The twining alders darken'd all the scene. (*a*)
Safe in the shade, the tenants of the wood
Assembled, bird and beast. The turtle-dove
Coo'd, amorous, all the livelong summer's day.
Lover of men, the piteous redbreast plain'd,
Sole-sitting on the bough. Blithe on the bush,
The blackbird, sweetest of the woodland choir,
Warbled his liquid lay ; to shepherd-swain
Mellifluous music, as his master's flock,
With his fair mistress and his faithful dog,
He tended in the vale : while leverets round,
In sportive races, through the forest flew
With feet of wind ; and, vent'ring from the rock,
The snow-white coney sought his ev'ning meal.
Here, too, the poet, as inspir'd at eve
He roam'd the dusky wood, or fabled brook
That piecemeal printed ruins in the rock,
Beheld the blue-eyed Sisters of the stream,
And heard the wild note of the fairy throng
That charm'd the Queen of heav'n, as round the tree
Time-hallow'd, hand in hand they led the dance,
With sky-blue mantles glitt'ring in her beam.

(*b*) Low by the Lake, as yet without a name,
Fair bosom'd in the bottom of the vale,
Arose a cottage, green with ancient turf,
Half hid in hoary trees, and from the north
Fenc'd by a wood, but open to the sun.
Here dwelt a peasant, rev'rend with the locks
Of age, yet youth was ruddy on his cheek ;

His farm his only care; his sole delight
To tend his daughter, beautiful and young,
To watch her paths, to fill her lap with flow'rs,
To see her spread into the bloom of years,
The perfect picture of her mother's youth.
His age's hope, the apple of his eye;
Belov'd of Heav'n, his fair Levina grew
In youth and grace, the Naiad of the vale.
Fresh as the flow'r amid the sunny show'rs
Of May, and blither than the bird of dawn,
Both roses' bloom gave beauty to her cheek,
Soft-temper'd with a smile. The light of heav'n,
And innocence, illum'd her virgin-eye,
Lucid and lovely as the morning star.
Her breast was fairer than the vernal bloom
Of valley-lily, op'ning in a show'r;
Fair as the morn, and beautiful as May,
The glory of the year, when first she comes
Array'd, all-beauteous, with the robes of heav'n,
And breathing summer breezes; from her locks
Shakes genial dews, and from her lap the flow'rs.
Thus beautiful she look'd; yet something more,
And better far than beauty, in her looks
Appear'd: the maiden blush of modesty;
The smile of cheerfulness, and sweet content;
Health's freshest rose, the sunshine of the soul;
Each height'ning each, effus'd o'er all her form
A nameless grace, the beauty of the mind.

  Thus finish'd fair above her peers, she drew
The eyes of all the village, and inflam'd
The rival shepherds of the neighb'ring dale,

Who laid the spoils of Summer at her feet,
And made the woods enamour'd of her name.
But pure as buds before they blow, and still
A virgin in her heart, she knew not love ;
But all alone, amid her garden fair,
From morn to noon, from noon to dewy eve,[1]
She spent her days ; her pleasing task to tend
The flow'rs ; to lave them from the water-spring ;
To ope the buds with her enamour'd breath,
Rank the gay tribes, and rear them in the sun.
In youth, the index of maturer years,
Left by her school-companions at their play,
She'd often wander in the wood, or roam
The wilderness, in quest of curious flow'r,
Or nest of bird unknown, till eve approach'd,
And hemm'd her in the shade.   To obvious swain,
Or woodman chanting in the greenwood glen,
She'd bring the beauteous spoils, and ask their names.
Thus ply'd assiduous her delightful task,
Day after day, till ev'ry herb she nam'd
That paints the robe of Spring, and knew the voice
Of every warbler in the vernal wood.

Her garden stretch'd along the river-side,
High up a sunny bank ; on either side,
A hedge forbade the vagrant foot ; above,
An ancient forest screen'd the green recess,
Transplanted here by her creative hand,

---

[1] Milton. Paradise Lost. Book i. p. 743.

> " From morn
> To noon he fell, from noon to dewy eve.
> A summer's day."

Each herb of Nature, full of fragrant sweets,
That scents the breath of summer; ev'ry flow'r,
Pride of the plain, that blooms on festal days
In shepherd's garland, and adorns the year,
In beauteous clusters flourish'd; Nature's work,
And order, finish'd by the hand of Art.
Here gowans, natives of the village green,
To daisies grew.   The lilies of the field
Put on the robe they neither sew'd nor spun.
Sweet-smelling shrubs and cheerful spreading trees,
Unfrequent scatter'd, as by Nature's hand,
Shaded the flow'rs, and to her Eden drew
The earliest concerts of the Spring, and all
The various music of the vocal year :
Retreat romantic !   Thus from early youth
Her life she led ; one summer's day, serene
And fair, without a cloud : like poet's dream
Of vernal landscapes, of Elysian vales,
And islands of the blest ; where, hand in hand,
Eternal Spring and Autumn rule the year,
And Love and Joy lead on immortal youth.

'Twas on a summer's day, when early show'rs
Had wak'd the various vegetable race
To life and beauty, fair Levina stray'd.
Far in the blooming wilderness she stray'd
To gather herbs, and the fair race of flow'rs,
That nature's hand creative pours at will,
Beauty unbounded ! over Earth's green lap,
Gay without number, in the day of rain.
O'er valleys gay, o'er hillocks green she walk'd,
Sweet as the season, and at times awak'd

The echoes of the vale, with native notes,
Of heart-felt joy, in numbers heav'nly sweet :
Sweet as th' hosannas of a Form of light,
A sweet-tongu'd Seraph in the bow'rs of bliss.

Her, as she halted on a green hill-top,
A quiver'd hunter spied.   Her flowing locks,
In golden ringlets glitt'ring to the sun,
Upon her bosom play'd : her mantle green.
Like thine, O Nature ! to her rosy cheek
Lent beauty new : as from the verdant leaf
The rose-bud blushes with a deeper bloom,
Amid the walks of May.   The stranger's eye
Was caught as with ethereal presence.   Oft
He look'd to heav'n, and oft he met her eye
In all the silent eloquence of love ;
Then, wak'd from wonder, with a smile began :
" Fair wanderer of the wood ! What heav'nly Pow'r.
Or Providence, conducts thy wand'ring steps
To this wild forest, from thy native seat
And parents. happy in a child so fair ?
A shepherdess, or virgin of the vale,
Thy dress bespeaks : but thy majestic mien.
And eye, bright as the morning-star, confess
Superior birth and beauty, born to rule :
As from the stormy cloud of night, that veils
Her virgin-orb, appears the Queen of heav'n,
And with full beauty, gilds the face of night.
Whom shall I call the fairest of her sex,
And charmer of my soul ?   In yonder vale.
Come, let us crop the roses of the brook,
And wildings of the wood : Soft under shade,

F

Let us recline by mossy fountain-side,
While the wood suffers in the beam of noon.
I 'll bring my love the choice of all the shades ;
First fruits ; the apple ruddy from the rock ;
And clust'ring nuts, that burnish in the beam.
O wilt thou bless my dwelling, and become
The owner of these fields ?   I 'll give thee all
That I possess, and all thou seest is mine."

Thus spoke the youth, with rapture in his eye,
And thus the maiden, with a blush began :
"Beyond the shadow of these mountains green,
Deep-bosom'd in the vale, a cottage stands,
The dwelling of my sire, a peaceful swain ;
Yet at his frugal board Health sits a guest,
And fair Contentment crowns his hoary hairs,
The patriarch of the plains : ne'er by his door
The needy pass'd, or the wayfaring man.
His only daughter, and his only joy,
I feed my father's flock ; and, while they rest,
At times retiring, lose me in the wood,
Skill'd in the virtues of each secret herb
That opes its virgin bosom to the Moon.
No flow'r amid the garden fairer grows
Than the sweet lily of the lowly vale,
The Queen of flow'rs--But sooner might the weed
That blooms and dies, the being of a day,
Presume to match with yonder mountain oak,
That stands the tempest and the bolt of heav'n,
From age to age the monarch of the wood——
O ! had you been a shepherd of the dale,
To feed your flock beside me, and to rest

With me at noon in these delightful shades,
I might have listened to the voice of love,
Nothing reluctant; might with you have walk'd
Whole summer-suns away. At eventide,
When heav'n and earth in all their glory shine
With the last smiles of the departing sun ;
When the sweet breath of Summer feasts the sense,
And secret pleasure thrills the heart of man ;
We might have walk'd alone, in converse sweet,
Along the quiet vale, and woo'd the Moon
To hear the music of true lovers' vows.
But fate forbids, and fortune's potent frown,
And honour, inmate of the noble breast.
Ne'er can this hand in wedlock join with thine.
Cease, beauteous stranger ! cease, beloved youth !
To vex a heart that never can be yours."

   Thus spoke the maid, deceitful : but her eyes,
Beyond the partial purpose of her tongue,
Persuasion gain'd. The deep-enamour'd youth
Stood gazing on her charms, and all his soul
Was lost in love. He grasped her trembling hand,
And breath'd the softest, the sincerest vows
Of love : "O virgin ! fairest of the fair !
My one beloved ! Were the Scottish throne
To me transmitted thro' a scepter'd line
Of ancestors, thou, thou shouldst be my Queen,
And Caledonia's diadems adorn
A fairer head than ever wore a crown."

   She redden'd like the morning, under veil
Of her own golden hair. The woods among,

They wander'd up and down with fond delay,
Nor mark'd the fall of ev'ning ; parted then,
The happiest pair on whom the sun declin'd.

Next day he found her on a flow'ry bank,
Half under shade of willows, by a spring,
The mirror of the swains, that o'er the meads,
Slow-winding, scatter'd flow'rets in its way.
Thro' many a winding walk and alley green,
She led him to her garden.   Wonder-struck,
He gaz'd, all eye, o'er th' enchanting scene :
And much he praised the walks, the groves, the flow'rs,
Her beautiful creation ; much he prais'd
The beautiful creatress ; and awak'd
The echo in her praise.   Like the first pair,
Adam and Eve in Eden's blissful bow'rs,
When newly come from their Creator's hand,
Our lovers liv'd in joy.   Here, day by day,
In fond endearments, in embraces sweet,
That lovers only know, they liv'd, they lov'd,
And found the paradise that Adam lost.
Nor did the virgin, with false modest pride,
Retard the nuptial morn : she fix'd the day
That bless'd the youth, and open'd to his eyes
An age of gold, the heav'n of happiness
That lovers in their lucid moments dream.

And now the Morning, like a rosy bride
Adorned on her day, put on her robes,
Her beauteous robes of light : the Naiad streams,
Sweet as the cadence of a poet's song,
Flow'd down the dale : the voices of the grove,

And ev'ry wingéd warbler of the air,
Sung over head, and there was joy in heav'n.
Ris'n with the dawn, the bride and bridal-maids
Stray'd thro' the woods, and o'er the vales, in quest
Of flow'rs, and garlands, and sweet-smelling herbs,
To strew the bridegroom's way, and deck his bed.

Fair in the bosom of the level Lake
Rose a green island, cover'd with a spring
Of flow'rs perpetual, goodly to the eye,
And blooming from afar.   High in the midst,
Between two fountains, an enchanted tree
Grew ever green, and every month renew'd
Its blooms and apples of Hesperian gold.
Here ev'ry bride (as ancient poets sing)
Two golden apples gather'd from the bough,
To give the bridegroom in the bed of love,
The pledge of nuptial concord and delight
For many a coming year.   Levina now
Had reach'd the isle, with an attendant maid,
And pull'd the mystic apples, pull'd the fruit;
But wish'd and long'd for the enchanted tree.
Not fonder sought the first created fair
The fruit forbidden of the mortal tree,
The source of human woe.   Two plants arose
Fair by the mother's side, with fruits and flow'rs
In miniature.   One, with audacious hand,
In evil hour [1] she rooted from the ground.
At once the island shook, and shrieks of woe
At times were heard, amid the troubled air.
Her whole frame shook, the blood forsook her face,

[1] Milton. Paradise Lost. B. ix. pp. 780-784.

Her knees knock'd, and her heart within her dy'd.
Trembling and pale, and boding woes to come,
They seized the boat, and hurried from the isle.

And now they gain'd the middle of the Lake,
And saw th' approaching land : now, wild with joy,
They row'd, they flew. When lo ! at once effus'd,
Sent by the angry demon of the isle,
A whirlwind rose : it lash'd the furious Lake
To tempest, overturn'd the boat, and sunk
The fair Levina to a wat'ry tomb.
Her sad companions, bending from a rock,
Thrice saw her head, and supplicating hands
Held up to heav'n, and heard the shriek of death :
Then overhead the parting billow closed,
And op'd no more. Her fate in mournful lays
The Muse relates ; and sure each tender maid
For her shall heave the sympathetic sigh,
And happ'ly my Eumelia [1] (for her soul
Is pity's self), as, void of household cares,
Her ev'ning walk she bends beside the Lake,
Which yet retains her name, shall sadly drop
A tear, in mem'ry of the hapless maid,
And mourn with me the sorrows of the youth,
Whom from his mistress death did not divide.
Robb'd of the calm possession of his mind,
All night he wander'd by the sounding shore,
Long looking o'er the Lake, and saw at times
The dear, the dreary ghost of her he lov'd ;
Till love and grief subdu'd his manly prime,
And brought his youth with sorrow to the grave.

[1] Eumelia. Magdalene Grieve. See Life, p. 25.

I knew an aged swain, whose hoary head
Was bent with years, the village chronicle,
Who much had seen, and from the former times
Much had received.   He, hanging o'er the hearth
In winter ev'nings, to the gaping swains,
And children circling round the fire, would tell
Stories of old, and tales of other times.
Of Lomond and Levina he would talk ;
And how of old, in Britain's evil days,
When brothers against brothers drew the sword
Of civil rage, the hostile hand of war
Ravag'd the land, gave cities to the sword,
And all the country to devouring fire.
Then these fair forests and Elysian scenes,
In one great conflagration, flam'd to heav'n.
Barren and black, by swift degrees arose
A muirish fen ; and hence the lab'ring hind,
Digging for fuel, meets the mould'ring trunks
Of oaks, and branchy antlers of the deer.

Now sober Industry, illustrious Power !
Hath rais'd the peaceful cottage, calm abode
Of Innocence and Joy : now, sweating, guides
The shining ploughshare ; tames the stubborn soil :
Leads the long drain along th' unfertile marsh ;
Bids the bleak hill with vernal verdure bloom,
The haunt of flocks : and clothes the barren heath
With waving harvests, and the golden grain.

Fair from his hand, behold the village rise,
In rural pride, 'mong intermingled trees !
Above whose aged tops, the joyful swains

At eventide, descending from the hill,
With eye enamour'd, mark the many wreaths
Of pillar'd smoke, high-curling to the clouds.
The street resounds with Labour's various voice,
Who whistles at his work.   Gay on the green,
Young blooming boys, and girls with golden hair,
Trip nimble-footed, wanton in their play,
The village hope.   All in a rev'rend row,
Their grey-haired grandsires, sitting in the sun,
Before the gate, and leaning on the staff,
The well-remember'd stories of their youth
Recount, and shake their aged locks with joy.

How fair a prospect rises to the eye,
Where beauty vies in all her vernal forms,
For ever pleasant, and for ever new !
Swells th' exulting thought, expands the soul,
Drowning each ruder care : a blooming train
Of bright ideas rushes on the mind.
Imagination rouses at the scene,
And backward, thro' the gloom of ages past,
Beholds Arcadia, like a rural Queen,
Encircled with her swains and rosy nymphs,
The mazy dance conducting on the green.
Nor yield to old Arcadia's blissful vales
Thine, gentle Leven ! green on either hand
Thy meadows spread, unbroken of the plough,
With beauty all their own.   Thy fields rejoice
With all the riches of the golden year.
Fat on the plain and mountain's sunny side,
Large droves of oxen, and the fleecy flocks
Feed undisturb'd, and fill the echoing air

With music, grateful to the master's ear.
The trav'ller stops, and gazes round and round
O'er all the scenes, that animate his heart
With mirth and music.   Even the mendicant,
Bowbent with age, that on the old grey stone,
Sole sitting, suns him in the public way,
Feels his heart leap, and to himself he sings.

   How beautiful around the Lake outspreads
Its wealth of waters, the surrounding vales
Renews, and holds a mirror to tke sky,
Perpetual fed by many sister streams,
Haunts of the angler !   First, the gulfy Po,
That thro' the quaking marsh and waving reeds
Creeps slow and silent on.   The rapid Queech,
Whose foaming torrents o'er the broken steep
Burst down impetuous, with the placid wave
Of flow'ry Leven, for the canine pike
And silver eel renown'd.   But chief thy stream,
O Gairny ! sweetly winding, claims the song.
First on thy banks the Doric reed I tun'd,
Stretch'd on the verdant grass ; while twilight meek,
Enrob'd in mist, slow-sailing thro' the air,
Silent and still, on ev'ry closéd flow'r
Shed drops nectareous ; and around the fields
No noise was heard, save where the whisp'ring reeds
Wav'd to the breeze, or in the dusky air
The slow wing'd crane mov'd heav'ly o'er the lea,
And shrilly clamour'd as he sought his nest.
There would I sit, and tune some youthful lay,
Or watch the motion of the living fires,
That day and night their never-ceasing course

Wheel round th' eternal poles, and bend the knee
To Him the Maker of yon starry sky,
Omnipotent! who, thron'd above all heav'ns,
Yet ever present through the peopl'd space
Of vast Creation's infinite extent,
Pours life, and bliss, and beauty, pours Himself,
His own essential goodness, o'er the minds
Of happy beings, thro' ten thousand worlds.

Nor shall the Muse forget thy friendly heart,
O Lelius![1] partner of my youthful hours;
How often, rising from the bed of peace,
We would walk forth to meet the summer morn,
Inhaling health and harmony of mind;
Philosophers and friends; while science beam'd
With ray divine as lovely on our minds
As yonder orient sun, whose welcome light
Reveal'd the vernal landscape to the view.
Yet oft, unbending from more serious thought,
Much of the looser follies of mankind,
Hum'rous and gay, we'd talk, and much would laugh;
While, ever and anon, their foibles vain
Imagination offer'd to our view.

(c) Fronting where Gairny pours his silent urn
Into the Lake, an island lifts its head
Grassy and wild, with ancient ruin heap'd
Of cells; where from the noisy world retir'd
Of old, as fame reports, Religion dwelt
Safe from the insults of the dark'ned crowd
That bow'd the knee to Odin; and in times

[1] Mr George Henderson, son of the Proprietor of Turfhills.

Of ignorance, when Caledonia's sons
(Before the triple-crownëd giant fell)
Exchang'd their simple faith for Rome's deceits.
Here Superstition for her cloister'd sons
A dwelling rear'd, with many an arched vault :
Where her pale vot'ries at the midnight-hour,
In many a mournful strain of melancholy,
Chanted their orisons to the cold moon.
It now resounds with the wild-shrieking gull,
The crested lapwing, and the clamorous mew.
The patient heron, and the bittern dull,
Deep-sounding in the base, with all the tribe
That by the water seek th' appointed meal.

From hence the shepherd in the fenced fold,
'Tis said, has heard strange sounds, and music wild ;
Such as in Selma, (d) by the burning oak
Of hero fallen, or of battle lost,
Warn'd Fingal's mighty son, from trembling chords
Of untouch'd harp, self-sounding in the night.
Perhaps th' afflicted Genius of the Lake,
That leaves the wat'ry grot, each night to mourn
The waste of time, his desolated isles
And temples in the dust : his plaintive voice
Is heard resounding thro' the dreary courts
Of high Lochleven Castle, (e) famous once,
Th' abode of heroes of the Bruce's line ;
Gothic the pile, and high the solid walls,
With warlike ramparts, and the strong defence
Of jutting battlements, an age's toil !
No more its arches echo to the noise
Of joy and festive mirth. No more the glance

Of blazing taper thro' its windows beams,
And quivers on the undulating wave:
But naked stand the melancholy walls,
Lash'd by the wintry tempests, cold and bleak,
That whistle mournful thro' the empty halls,
And piecemeal crumble down the tow'rs to dust.
Perhaps in some lone, dreary, desert tower,
That time has spar'd, forth from the window looks,
Half hid in grass, the solitary fox;
While from above, the owl, musician dire!
Screams hideous, harsh, and grating to the ear.

Equal in age, and sharers of its fate,
A row of moss-grown trees around it stand.
Scarce here and there, upon their blasted tops,
A shrivell'd leaf distinguishes the year;
Emblem of hoary age, the eve of life,
When man draws nigh his everlasting home,
Within a step of the devouring grave;
When all his views and tow'ring hopes are gone,
And ev'ry appetite before him dead.

Bright shines the morn, while in the ruddy east
The sun hangs hov'ring o'er the Atlantic wave.
Apart, on yonder green hill's sunny side,
Seren'd with all the music of the morn,
Attentive let me sit; while from the rock,
The swains, laborious, roll the limestone huge,
Bounding elastic from th' indented grass,
At every fall it springs, and thund'ring shoots,
O'er rocks and precipices, to the plain.
And let the shepherd careful tend his flock

Far from the dang'rous steep ; nor, O ye swains !
Stray heedless of its rage. Behold the tears
Yon wretched widow o'er the mangled corpse
Of her dead husband pours, who, hapless man !
Cheerful and strong went forth at rising morn
To usual toil ; but, ere the evening hour,
His sad companions bare him lifeless home.
Urg'd from the hill's high top, with progress swift,
A weighty stone, resistless, rapid came.
Seen by the fated wretch, who stood unmov'd.
Nor turn'd to fly, till flight had been in vain ;
When now arriv'd the instrument of death,
And fell'd him to the ground. The thirsty land
Drank up his blood : such was the will of Heav'n..

How wide the landscape opens to the view !
Still as I mount, the less'ning hills decline,
Till high above them northern Grampius lifts
His hoary head, bending beneath a load
Of everlasting snow. O'er southern fields
I see the Cheviot hills, the ancient bounds
Of two contending kingdoms. There in fight
Brave Percy and the gallant Douglas bled,
The house of heroes, and the death of hosts !
Wat'ring the fertile fields, majestic Forth,
Full, deep, and wide, rolls placid to the sea,
With many a vessel trim and oared bark
In rich profusion cover'd, wafting o'er
The wealth and product of far distant lands.

But chief mine eye on the subjected vale
Of Leven pleas'd looks down ; while o'er the trees.

That shield the hamlet with the shade of years,
The tow'ring smoke of early fire ascends,
And the shrill cock proclaims th' advancéd morn.

How blest the man ! who, in these peaceful plains,
Ploughs his paternal field ; far from the noise,
The care, and bustle of a busy world.
All in the sacred, sweet, sequester'd vale
Of Solitude, the secret primrose-path
Of rural life, he dwells ; and with him dwells
Peace and Content, twins of the sylvan shade,
And all the Graces of the golden age.
Such is Agricola, the wise, the good,
By nature forméd for the calm retreat,
The silent path of life.   Learn'd, but not fraught
With self-importance, as the starchéd fool ;
Who challenges respect by solemn face,
By studied accent, and high-sounding phrase.
Enamour'd of the shade, but not morose.
Politeness, rais'd in courts by frigid rules,
With him spontaneous grows.   Not books alone,
But man his study, and the better part ;
To tread the ways of virtue, and to act
The various scenes of life with God's applause.
Deep in the bottom of the flow'ry vale,
With blooming sallows and the leafy twine
Of verdant alders fenc'd, his dwelling stands
Complete in rural elegance.   The door,
By which the poor or pilgrim never pass'd,
Still open, speaks the master's bounteous heart.
There, O how sweet ! amid the fragrant shrubs
At ev'ning cool to sit ; while, on their boughs,

The nested songsters twitter o'er their young.
And the hoarse low of folded cattle breaks
The silence, wafted o'er the sleeping Lake,
Whose waters glow beneath the purple tinge
Of western cloud ; while converse sweet deceives
The stealing foot of time.   Or where the ground,
Mounded irregular, points out the graves
Of our forefathers, and the hallow'd fane,
Where swains assembling worship, let us walk,
In softly-soothing melancholy thought,
As Night's seraphic bard, immortal Young,
Or sweet-complaining Gray : there see the goal
Of human life, where drooping, faint, and tir'd,
Oft miss'd the prize,—the weary racer rests.

Thus sung the youth, amid unfertile wilds
And nameless deserts, unpoetic ground !
Far from his friends he stray'd, recording thus
The dear remembrance of his native fields,
To cheer the tedious night ; while slow disease
Prey'd on his pining vitals, and the blasts
Of chill December shook his humble cot.

THE LAST DAY.

A POEM.

Bruce composed this poem as an exercise or essay for one of the meetings of the Edinburgh University Literary Society. Dr MacKelvie tells us how, as he drew near the close of his last illness, " He abandoned writing upon other subjects, and confined himself to the improvement of his poem on 'The Last Day,' to which it is known he added a number of verses, the greater part of which, in its improved state, he transferred into his volume of MSS., but he was not allowed to finish it."

The fascination of this august theme for the devout spirit is evidenced by the marvellous story and popularity of the well-known hymn. "Dies Iræ," which has lived over at least some five centuries, been translated and paraphrased beyond reckoning, and entered so largely into the religious worship of Christendom.

HIS second coming, who at first appeared
To save the world, but now to judge mankind
According to their works ;—the trumpet's sound,—
The dead arising,--the wide world in flames.--
The mansions of the blest, and the dire pit
Of Satan and of woe,——O Muse ! unfold.
    O Thou ! whose eye the future and the past
In one broad view beholdest—from the first
Of days, when o'er this rude unformed mass
Light, first-born of existence, smiling rose,
Down to that latest moment, when thy voice
Shall bid the sun be darkness, when thy hand
Shall blot creation out,—assist my song !
Thou only know'st, who gav'st these orbs to roll

Their destin'd circles, when their course shall set ;
When ruin and destruction fierce shall ride
In triumph o'er creation. This is hid,
In kindness unto man. Thou giv'st to know
The event certain : angels know not when.
   'Twas on an autumn's eve, serene and calm,
I walked, attendant on the funeral
Of an old swain : around, the village crowd
Loquacious chatted, till we reach'd the place
Where, shrouded up, the sons of other years
Lie silent in the grave. The sexton there
Had digg'd the bed of death, the narrow house,
For all that live, appointed. To the dust
We gave the dead. Then moralizing, home
The swains return'd, to drown in copious bowls
The labours of the day, and thoughts of death.
   The sun now trembled at the western gate :
His yellow rays stream'd in the fleecy clouds.
I sat me down upon a broad flat stone :
And much I mused on the changeful state
Of sublunary things. The joys of life,
How frail, how short, how passing ! As the sea,
Now flowing, thunders on the rocky shore ;
Now lowly ebbing, leaves a tract of sand,
Waste, wide, and dreary : so, in this vain world,
Through every varying state of life, we toss
In endless fluctuation ; till, tir'd out
With sad variety of bad and worse,
We reach life's period, reach the blissful port,
Where change affects not, and the weary rest.
   Then sure the sun which lights us to our shroud,
Than that which gave us first to see the light.

G

Is happier far. As he who, hopeless, long
Hath rode th' Atlantic billow, from the mast,
Skirting the blue horizon, sees the land,
His native land, approach ; joy fills his heart,
And swells each throbbing vein : so, here confin'd,
We weary tread life's long, long toilsome maze ;
Still hoping, vainly hoping, for relief,
And rest from labour. Ah ! mistaken thought :
To seek in life what only death can give.
But what is death ? Is it an endless sleep,
Unconscious of the present and the past,
And never to be waken'd ? Sleeps the soul ;
Nor wakes ev'n in a dream ? If it is so,
Happy the sons of pleasure ; they have liv'd
And made the most of life : and foolish he,
The sage, who, dreaming of hereafter, grudg'd
Himself the tasting of the sweets of life,
And call'd it temperance ; and hop'd for joys
More durable and sweet, beyond the grave.
Vain is the poet's song, the soldier's toil !
Vain is the sculptur'd marble and the bust !
How vain to hope for never-dying fame,
If souls can die ! But that they never die,
This thirst of glory whispers. Wherefore gave
The great Creator such a strong desire
He never meant to satisfy ? These stones,
Memorials of the dead, with rustic art
And rude inscription cut, declare the soul
Immortal. Man, form'd for eternity,
Abhors annihilation, and the thought
Of dark oblivion. Hence, with ardent wish
And vigorous effort, each would fondly raise

Some lasting monument, to save his name
Safe from the waste of years.   Hence Cæsar fought;
Hence Raphael painted; and hence Milton sung.
   Thus musing, sleep oppress'd my drowsy sense,
And wrapt me into rest.   Before mine eyes,
Fair as the morn, when up the flaming east
The sun ascends, a radiant seraph stood,
Crown'd with a wreath of palm : his golden hair
Wav'd on his shoulders, girt with shining plumes ;
From which, down to the ground, loose-floating trail'd,
In graceful negligence, his heavenly robe :
Upon his face, flush'd with immortal youth,
Unfading beauty bloom'd ; and thus he spake :
   " Well hast thou judged ; the soul must be immortal !
And that it is, this awful day declares ;
This day, the last that e'er the sun shall gild :
Arrested by Omnipotence, no more
Shall he describe the year : the moon no more
Shall shed her borrow'd light.   This is the day
Seal'd in the rolls of Fate, when o'er the dead
Almighty Power shall wake and raise to life
The sleeping myriads.   Now shall be approv'd
The ways of God to man, and all the clouds
Of Providence be clear'd : now shall be disclos'd
Why vice in purple oft upon a throne
Exalted sat, and shook her iron scourge
O'er virtue, lowly seated on the ground :
Now deeds committed in the sable shade
Of eyeless darkness, shall be brought to light ;
And every act shall meet its just reward."
   As thus he spake, the morn arose ; and sure
Methought ne'er rose a fairer.   Not a cloud

Spotted the blue expanse ; and not a gale
Breath'd o'er the surface of the dewy earth.
Twinkling with yellow lustre, the gay birds
On every blooming spray sung their sweet lays,
And praised their great Creator : through the fields
The lowing cattle graz'd ; and all around
Was beauty, happiness, and mirth, and love.—
"All these thou seest (resum'd the angelic power)
No more shall give thee pleasure.   Thou must leave
This world ; of which now come and see the end."
    This said, he touch'd me, and such strength infus'd,
That as he soared up the pathless air,
I lightly followed.   On the awful peak
Of an eternal rock, against whose base
The sounding billows beat, he set me down.
I heard a noise, loud as a rushing stream,
When o'er the rugged precipice it roars,
And foaming, thunders on the rocks below.
Astonished, I gaz'd around ; when lo !
I saw an angel down from Heaven descend.
His face was as the sun ; his dreadful height
Such as the statue, by the Grecian plan'd,
Of Philip's son, Athos, with all his rocks,
Moulded into a man : One foot on earth,
And one upon the rolling sea, he fix'd.
As when, at setting sun, the rainbow shines
Refulgent, meting out the half of Heav'n—
So stood he ; and, in act to speak he rais'd
His shining hand.   His voice was as the sound
Of many waters, or the deep-mouth'd roar
Of thunder, when it bursts the riven cloud,
And bellows through the ether.   Nature stood

Silent, in all her works : while thus he spake :—
"Hear, thou that roll'st above, thou radiant sun !
Ye heavens and earth, attend ! while I declare
The will of the Eternal. By His name
Who lives, and shall for ever live, I swear
That time shall be no longer."
    He disappear'd. Fix'd in deep thought I stood,
At what would follow. Straight another sound ;
To which the Nile, o'er Ethiopia's rocks
Rushing in one broad cataract, were nought.
It seem'd as if the pillars that upheld
The universe had fall'n ; and all its worlds,
Unhing'd, had strove together for the way,
In cumbrous crashing ruin. Such the roar !
A sound that might be felt ! It pierc'd beyond
The limits of creation. Chaos roar'd ;
And heav'n and earth return'd the mighty noise.—
"Thou hear'st," said then my heav'nly guide, "the sound
Of the last trumpet. See, where from the clouds
Th' archangel Michael, one of the seven
That minister before the throne of God,
Leans forward ; and the sonorous tube inspires
With breath immortal. By his side the sword
Which, like a meteor, o'er the vanquished head
Of Satan hung, when he rebellious rais'd
War, and embroil'd the happy fields above."
    A pause ensued. The fainting sun grew pale,
And seem'd to struggle through a sky of blood ;
While dim eclipse impair'd his beam : the earth
Shook to her deepest centre ; Ocean rag'd,
And dash'd his billows on the frighted shore.
All was confusion. Heartless, helpless, wild,

As flocks of timid sheep, or driven deer,
Wandering, th' inhabitants of earth appear'd :
Terror in every look, and pale affright
Sat in each eye ; amazed at the past,
And for the future trembling.   All call'd great,
Or deem'd illustrious, by erring man,
Was now no more.   The hero and the prince,
Their grandeur lost, now mingled with the crowd ;
And all distinctions, those except from faith
And virtue flowing : these upheld the soul,
As ribb'd with triple steel.   All else were lost !
  Now, vain is greatness ! as the morning clouds,
That, rising, promise rain : condens'd they stand,
Till, touch'd by winds, they vanish into air.
The farmer mourns : so mourns the helpless wretch,
Who, cast by fortune from some envied height,
Finds nought within him to support his fall.
High as his hopes had rais'd him, low he sinks
Below his fate, in comfortless despair.——
Who would not laugh at an attempt to build
A lasting structure on the rapid stream
Of foaming Tigris, the foundations laid
Upon the glassy surface ?   Such the hopes
Of him whose views are bounded to this world :
Immers'd in his own labour'd work, he dreams
Himself secure ; when, on a sudden, down,
Torn from its sandy ground, the fabric falls !
He starts, and, waking, finds himself undone.
  Not so the man who on religion's base
His hope and virtue founds.   Firm on the Rock
Of ages his foundation laid, remains,
Above the frowns of fortune or her smiles ;

In every varying state of life, the same.
Nought fears he from the world, and nothing hopes.
With unassuming courage, inward strength
Endu'd, resign'd to Heaven, he leads a life
Superior to the common herd of men,
Whose joys, connected with the changeful flood
Of fickle fortune, ebb and flow with it.
   Nor is religion a chimera : Sure
'Tis something real. Virtue cannot live,
Divided from it. As a sever'd branch
It withers, pines, and dies. Who loves not God,
That made him, and preserv'd, nay more—redeem'd.
Is dangerous. Can ever gratitude
Bind him who spurns at these most sacred ties ?
Say, can he, in the silent scenes of life,
Be sociable ? Can he be a friend ?
At best, he must but feign. The worst of brutes
An atheist is ; for beasts acknowledge God.
The lion, with the terrors of his mouth,
Pays homage to his Maker ; the grim wolf,
At midnight, howling, seeks his meat from God.
   Again th' archangel raised his dreadful voice.
Earth trembled at the sound. "Awake, ye dead !
And come to judgment." At the mighty call,
As armies issue at the trumpet's sound,
So rose the dead. A shaking first I heard,
And bone together came unto his bone,
Though sever'd by wide seas and distant lands.
A spirit liv'd within them. He who made,
Wound up, and set in motion, the machine,
To run unhurt the length of fourscore years,
Who knows the structure of each secret spring ;

Can He not join again the sever'd parts,
And join them with advantage ?　This to man
Hard and impossible may seem ; to God
Is easy.　Now, through all the darken'd air,
The living atoms flew, each to his place,
And nought was missing in the great account,
Down from the dust of him whom Cain first slew,
To him who yesterday was laid in earth,
And scarce had seen corruption ; whether in
The bladed grass they cloth'd the verdant plain,
Or smil'd in opening flowers ; or, in the sea,
Became the food of monsters of the Deep,
Or pass'd in transmigrations infinite
Through ev'ry kind of being.　None mistakes
His kindred matter ; but by sympathy
Combining, rather by Almighty Pow'r
Led on, they closely mingle and unite,
But chang'd : for subject to decay no more,
Or dissolution, deathless as the soul,
The body is ; and fitted to enjoy
Eternal bliss, or bear eternal pain.

　　As when in Spring the sun's prolific beams
Have wak'd to life the insect tribes, that sport
And wanton in his rays at ev'ning mild,
Proud of their new existence, up the air,
In devious circles wheeling, they ascend,
Innumerable ; the whole air is dark :
So, by the trumpet rous'd, the sons of men,
In countless numbers, cover'd all the ground,
From frozen Greenland to the southern pole ;
All who ere liv'd on earth.　See Lapland's sons,
Whose zenith is the pole ; a barb'rous race !

Rough as their storms, and savage as their clime,
Unpolish'd as their bears, and but in shape
Distinguish'd from them : Reason's dying lamp
Scarce brighter burns than instinct in their breast.
With wand'ring Russians, and all those who dwelt
In Scandinavia, by the Baltic Sea ;
The rugged Pole, with Prussia's warlike race :
Germania pours her numbers, where the Rhine
And mighty Danube pour their flowing urns.
   Behold thy children, Britain ! hail the light :
A manly race, whose business was arms,
And long uncivilised ; yet, train'd to deeds
Of virtue, they withstood the Roman power,
And made their eagles droop. On Morven's coast
A race of heroes and of bards arise,
The mighty Fingal, and his mighty son,
Who launch'd the spear, and touch'd the tuneful harp ;
With Scotia's chiefs, the sons of later years,
Her Kenneths and her Malcolms, warriors fam'd ;
Her generous Wallace, and her gallant Bruce.
See, in her pathless wilds, where the grey stones
Are raised in memory of the mighty dead,
Armies arise of English, Scots, and Picts ;
And giant Danes, who, from bleak Norway's coast,
Ambitious, came to conquer her fair fields,
And chain her sons : But Scotia gave them graves !—
Behold the kings that fill'd the English throne !
Edwards and Henries, names of deathless fame,
Start from the tomb. Immortal William ! see,
Surrounding angels point him from the rest,
Who saved the State from tyranny and Rome.
Behold her poets ! Shakespeare, fancy's child ;

Spencer. who. through his smooth and moral tale.
Y-points fair virtue out ; with him who sung
Of man's first disobedience.   Young lifts up
His awful head, and joys to see the day,
The great. th' important day, of which he sung.
　See where imperial Rome exalts her height :
Her senators and gowned fathers rise ;
Her consuls, who. as ants without a king.
Went forth to conquer kings : and at their wheels
In triumph led the chiefs of distant lands.
Behold. in Cannæ's field. what hostile swarms
Burst from th' ensanguin'd ground, where Hannibal
Shook Rome through all her legions : Italy
Trembled unto the Capitol.   If fate
Had not withstood th' attempt, she now had bow'd
Her head to Carthage.   See, Pharsalia pours
Her murder'd thousands ! who, in the last strife
Of Rome for dying liberty, were slain,
To make a man the master of the world.
　All Europe's sons throng forward ; numbers vast !
Imagination fails beneath the weight.
What numbers yet remain !   Th' enervate race
Of Asia. from where Tanais rolls
O'er rocks and dreary wastes his foaming stream.
To where the Eastern Ocean thunders round
The spicy Java ; with the tawny race
That dwelt in Afric. from the Red Sea, north.
To the Cape, south. where the rude Hottentot
Sinks into brute ; with those, who long unknown
Till by Columbus found, a naked race !
And only skill'd to urge the sylvan war,
That peopled the wide continent that spreads

From rocky Zembla, whiten'd with the snow
Of twice three thousand years, south to the Straits
Nam'd from Magellan, where the ocean roars
Round earth's remotest bounds. Now, had not He,
The great Creator of the universe,
Enlarg'd the wide foundations of the world,
Room had been wanting to the mighty crowds
That pour'd from every quarter. At His word,
Obedient angels stretch'd an ample plain,
Where dwelt His people in the Holy Land,
Fit to contain the whole of human race——
As when the autumn, yellow on the fields,
Invites the sickle, forth the farmer sends
His servants to cut down and gather in
The bearded grain: so, by Jehovah sent,
His angels, from all corners of the world,
Led on the living and awaken'd dead
To judgment : as, in th' Apocalypse,
John gather'd, saw the people of the earth,
And kings, to Armageddon.——Now look round
Thou whose ambitious heart for glory beats !
See all the wretched things on earth call'd great,
And lifted up to gods ! How little now
Seems all their grandeur ! See the conqueror,
Mad Alexander, who his victor arms
Bore o'er the then known globe, then sat him down
And wept, because he had no other world
To give to desolation : how he droops !
He knew not, hapless wretch ! he never learn'd
The harder conquest—to subdue himself.
Now is the Christian's triumph, now he lifts
His head on high : while down the dying hearts

Of sinners helpless sink : black guilt distracts
And wrings their tortur'd souls ; while every thought
Is big with keen remorse, or dark despair.
    But now a nobler subject claims the song.
My mind recoils at the amazing theme :
For how shall finite speak of infinite ?
How shall a stripling, by the Muse untaught,
Sing Heaven's Almighty, prostrate at whose feet
Archangels fall ? Unequal to the task,
I dare the bold attempt : assist me, Heaven !
From Thee begun, with Thee shall end my song !
    Now, down from th' opening firmament,
Seated upon a sapphire throne, high rais'd
Upon an azure ground, upheld by wheels
Of emblematic structure, as a wheel
Had been within a wheel, studded with eyes
Of flaming fire, and by four cherubs led ;
I saw the Judge descend. Around Him came
By thousands and by millions, Heaven's bright host.
About Him blaz'd insufferable light,
Invisible as darkness to the eye.
His car above the mount of Olives stay'd
Where last with His disciples He convers'd,
And left them gazing as He soar'd aloft.
He darkness as a curtain drew around ;
On which the colour of the rainbow shone,
Various and bright ; and from within was heard
A voice, as deep-mouth'd thunder, speaking thus :
"Go, Raphael, and from these reprobate
Divide my chosen saints ; go separate
My people from among them, as the wheat
Is in the harvest sever'd from the tares :

Set them upon the right, and on the left
Leave these ungodly. Thou, Michael, choose.
From forth th' angelic host, a chosen band,
And Satan with his legions hither bring
To judgment, from Hell's caverns ; whither fled.
They think to hide from my awaken'd wrath,
Which chas'd them out of Heaven, and which they dread
More than the horrors of the pit, which now
Shall be redoubled sevenfold on their heads."
   Swift as conception, at His bidding flew
His ministers, obedient to His word.
And, as a shepherd, who all day hath fed
His sheep and goats promiscuous, but at eve
Dividing, shuts them up in different folds :
So now the good were parted from the bad ;
For ever parted ; never more to join
And mingle as on earth, where often past
For other each ; ev'n close Hypocrisy
Escapes not, but, unmask'd, alike the scorn
Of vice and virtue stands. Now separate,
Upon the right appear'd a dauntless, firm,
Composed number : joyful at the thought
Of immortality, they forward look'd
With hope unto the future ; conscience, pleas'd,
Smiling, reflects upon a well-spent life ;
Heaven dawns within their breasts. The other crew,
Pale and dejected, scarcely lift their heads
To view the hated light : his trembling hand
Each lays upon his guilty face ; and now,
In gnawings of the never-dying worm,
Begins a hell that never shall be quench'd.
   But now the enemy of God and man,

Cursing his fate, comes forward, led in chains,
Infrangible, of burning adamant,
Hewn from the rocks of Hell; now too the bands
Of rebel angels, who long time had walk'd
The world, and by their oracles deceiv'd
The blinded nations, or by secret guile
Wrought men to vice, came on, raging in vain,
And struggling with their fetters, which, as fate,
Compell'd them fast. They wait their dreadful doom.
  Now from His lofty throne, with eyes that blaz'd
Intolerable day, th' Almighty Judge
Look'd down awhile upon the subject crowd.
As when a caravan of merchants, led
By thirst of gain to travel the parch'd sands
Of waste Arabia, hears a lion roar,
The wicked trembled at His view; upon
The ground they roll'd, in pangs of wild despair,
To hide their faces, which not blushes mark'd
But livid horror. Conscience, who asleep
Long time had lain, now lifts her snaky head,
And frights them into madness; while the list
Of all their sins she offers to their view:
For she had power to hurt them, and her sting
Was as a scorpion's. He who never knew
Its wound is happy, though a fetter'd slave,
Chain'd to the oar, or to the dark damp mine
Confin'd; while he who sits upon a throne,
Under her frown, is wretched. But the damn'd
Alone can tell what 'tis to feel her scourge
In all its horrors, with her poison'd sting
Fix'd in their hearts. This is the Second Death.
  Upon the Book of Life He laid His hand,

Clos'd with the seal of Heaven ; which op'd, He read
The names of the Elect. GOD knows His own.
"Come (looking on the right, He mildly said),
Ye of my Father blessed, ere the world
Was moulded out of chaos—ere the sons
Of GOD, exulting, sung at Nature's birth :
For you I left my throne, my glory left,
And, shrouded up in clay, I weary walk'd
Your world, and many miseries endur'd :
Death was the last. For you I died, that you
Might live with me for ever, and in Heav'n sit
On thrones, and as the sun in brightness, shine
For ever in my kingdom. Faithfully
Have ye approv'd yourselves. I hungry was,
And thirsty, and ye gave me meat and drink ;
Ye clothed me, naked ; when I fainting lay
In all the sad variety of pain,
Ye cheer'd me with the tenderness of friends ;
In sickness and in prison, me reliev'd.
Nay, marvel not that thus I speak : whene'er,
Led by the dictates of fair charity,
Ye help'd the man on whom keen poverty
And wretchedness had laid their meagre hands,
And for my sake, ye did it unto me."
    They heard with joy, and, shouting, rais'd their voice
In praise of their Redeemer ! Loos'd from earth,
They soar'd triumphant, and at the right hand
Of the great Judge sat down ; who on the left
Now looking stern, with fury in His eyes,
Blasted their spirits, while His arrows fix'd
Deep in the hearts, in agonizing pain
Scorched their vitals, thus their dreadful doom

(More dreadful from those lips which us'd to bless)
He awfully pronounc'd.   Earth at His frown
Convulsive trembled ; while the raging deep
Hush'd in a horrid calm his waves.   "Depart,"
(These, for I heard them, were His awful words !)
"Depart from me, ye cursed !   Oft have I strove,
In tenderness and pity, to subdue
Your rebel hearts ; as a fond parent bird,
When danger threatens, flutters round her young,
Nature's strong impulse beating in her breast.
Thus ardent did I strive : But all in vain.
Now will I laugh at your calamity,
And mock your fears : as oft, in stupid mirth,
Harden'd in wickedness, ye pointed out
The man who labour'd up the steep ascent
Of virtue, to reproach.   Depart to fire
Kindled in Tophet for th' arch enemy,
For Satan and his angels, who, by pride,
Fell into condemnation ; blown up now
To sevenfold fury by th' Almighty breath.
There, in that dreary mansion, where the light
Is solid gloom, darkness that may be felt,
Where hope, the lenient of the ills of life,
For ever dies ; there shall ye seek for death,
And shall not find it : for your greatest curse
Is immortality.   Omnipotence
Eternally shall punish and preserve."
   So said He ; and, His hand high lifting, hurl'd
The flashing lightning, and the flaming bolt.
Full on the wicked : kindling in a blaze
The scorched earth.   Behind, before, around,
The trembling wretches, burst the quiv'ring flames.

They turn'd to fly ; but wrath divine pursu'd
To where, beyond creation's utmost bound,
Where never glimpse of cheerful light arriv'd.
Where scarce e'en thought can travel, but, absorb'd,
Falls headlong down th' immeasurable gulf
Of Chaos—wide and wild, their prison stood
Of utter darkness, as the horrid shade
That clouds the brow of death. Its op'ned mouth
Belch'd sheets of livid flame and pitchy smoke.
Infernal thunders, with explosion dire,
Roar'd through the fiery concave ; while the waves
Of liquid sulphur beat the burning shore,
In endless ferment. O'er the dizzy steep
Suspended, wrapt in suffocating gloom,
The sons of black damnation shrieking hung.
Curses unutterable filled their mouths,
Hideous to hear ; their eyes rain'd bitter tears
Of agonizing madness, for their day
Was past, and from their eye repentance hid
For ever ! Round their heads their hissing brands
The Furies wav'd, and o'er the whelming brink
Impetuous urg'd them. In the boiling surge
They headlong fell. The flashing billows roar'd :
And hell from all her caves return'd the sound.
The gates of flint, and tenfold adamant,
With bars of steel, impenetrably firm,
Were shut for ever : The decree of fate,
Immutable, made fast the pond'rous door.
    "Now turn thine eyes," my bright conductor said :
"Behold the world in flames ! so sore the bolts
Of thunder, launch'd by the Almighty arm,
Hath smote upon it. Up the blacken'd air

II

Ascend the curling flames, and billowy smoke ;
And hideous crackling, blot the face of day
With foul eruption.   From their inmost beds
The hissing waters rise.   Whatever drew
The vital air, or in the spacious deep
Wanton'd at large, expires.   Heard'st thou that crash ?
There fell the tow'ring Alps, and, dashing down,
Lay bare their centre.   See, the flaming mines
Expand their treasures ! no rapacious hand
To seize the precious bane.   Now look around :
Say, Canst thou tell where stood imperial Rome,
The wonder of the world ; or where, the boast
Of Europe, fair Britannia, stretch'd her plain,
Encircled by the ocean ?   All is wrapt
In darkness : as (if great may be compar'd
With small) when, on Gomorrah's fated field,
The flaming sulphur, by Jehovah rain'd,
Sent up a pitchy cloud, killing to life,
And tainting all the air.   Another groan !
'Twas Nature's last : and see ! th' extinguish'd sun
Falls devious through the void ; and the fair face
Of nature is no more !   With sullen joy
Old Chaos views the havoc, and expects
To stretch his sable sceptre o'er the blank
Where once Creation smil'd : o'er which, perhaps,
Creative energy again shall wake,
And into being call a brighter sun,
And fairer worlds ; which, for delightful change,
The Saints, descending from the happy seats
Of bliss, shall visit.   And behold ! they rise,
And seek their native land : around them move,
In radiant files, Heaven's host.   Immortal wreaths

Of amaranth and roses crown their heads ;
And each a branch of ever-blooming palm
Triumphant holds.   In robes of dazzling white,
Fairer than that by wintry tempests shed
Upon the frozen ground, array'd, they shine,
Fair as the sun, when up the steep of Heav'n
He rides in all the majesty of light.
   But who can tell, or if an angel could,
Thou couldst not hear, the glories of the place
For their abode prepar'd ?   Though oft on earth
They struggled hard against the stormy tide
Of adverse fortune, and the bitter scorn
Of harden'd villainy—their life a course
Of warfare upon earth ; these toils, when view'd
With the reward, seem nought.   The LORD shall guide
Their steps to living fountains, and shall wipe
All tears from ev'ry eye.   The wintry clouds
That frown'd on life, rack up.   A glorious sun,
That ne'er shall set, arises in a sky
Unclouded and serene.   Their joy is full :
And sickness, pain, and death, shall be no more.
   Dost thou desire to follow ? does thy heart
Beat ardent for the prize ?   Then tread the path
Religion points to man.   What thou hast seen,
Fix'd in thy heart retain : For, be assur'd,
In that last moment—in the closing act
Of Nature's drama, ere the hand of fate
Drop the black curtain, thou must bear thy part,
And stand in thine own lot——"

                    This said, he stretch'd
His wings, and in a moment left my sight.

II.

Ode: To the Cuckoo

and

Elegy: To Spring.

ODE:

TO THE CUCKOO.[1]

I.

HAIL, beauteous Stranger of the wood !
  Attendant on the Spring !
Now heav'n repairs thy rural seat,
  And woods thy welcome sing.

II.

Soon as the daisy decks the green,
  Thy certain voice we hear :
Hast thou a star to guide thy path,
  Or mark the rolling year ?

III.

Delightful visitant ! with thee
  I hail the time of flow'rs,
When heav'n is fill'd with music sweet
  Of birds among the bow'rs.

IV.

The schoolboy wand'ring in the wood
  To pull the flow'rs so gay,
Starts, thy curious voice to hear,
  And imitates thy lay.

[1] See Writings, p. 35 ; Appendix A ; also Notes to the Poems (*g*).

V.

Soon as the pea puts on the bloom,
    Thou fly'st thy vocal vale,
An annual guest, in other lands,
    Another Spring to hail.

VI.

Sweet bird! thy bow'r is ever green,
    Thy sky is ever clear;
Thou hast no sorrow in thy song,
    No winter in thy year!

VII.

Alas! sweet bird! not so my fate,
    Dark scowling skies I see
Fast gathering round, and fraught with woe
    And wintry years to me.

VIII.

O could I fly, I'd fly with thee:
    We'd make, with social wing,
Our annual visit o'er the globe,
    Companions of the Spring.

ELEGY:

TO SPRING.[1]

'TIS past: the iron North has spent his rage;
  Stern Winter now resigns the length'ning day;
The stormy howlings of the winds asswage,
  And warm o'er ether western breezes play.

Of genial heat and cheerful light the source,
  From southern climes, beneath another sky,
The sun, returning, wheels his golden course;
  Before his beams all noxious vapours fly.

Far to the north grim Winter draws his train
  To his own clime, to ZEMBLA'S frozen shore;
Where, thron'd on ice, he holds eternal reign;
  Where whirlwinds madden, and where tempests roar.

Loos'd from the bands of frost, the verdant ground
  Again puts on her robe of cheerful green,
Again puts forth her flow'rs; and all around,
  Smiling, the cheerful face of Spring is seen.

Behold! the trees new-deck their wither'd boughs:
  Their ample leaves the hospitable plane,
The taper elm, and lofty ash, disclose;
  The blooming hawthorn variegates the scene.

[1] See Writings, p. 52.

The lily of the vale, of flow'rs the Queen,
  Puts on the robe she neither sew'd nor spun :
The birds on ground, or on the branches green,
  Hop to and fro, and glitter in the sun.

Soon as o'er eastern hills the morning peers,
  From her low nest the tufted lark upsprings ;
And, cheerful singing, up the air she steers ;
  Still high she mounts, still loud and sweet she sings.

On the green furze, cloth'd o'er with golden blooms
  That fill the air with fragrance all around,
The linnet sits, and tricks his glossy plumes,
  While o'er the wild his broken notes resound.

While the sun journeys down the western sky,
  Along the greensward, mark'd with ROMAN mound,
Beneath the blithesome shepherd's watchful eye,
  The cheerful lambkins dance and frisk around.

Now is the time for those who wisdom love,
  Who love to walk in Virtue's flow'ry road,
Along the lovely paths of Spring to rove,
  And follow Nature up to Nature's GOD.

Thus ZOROASTER studied Nature's laws ;
  Thus SOCRATES, the wisest of mankind ;
Thus heav'n-taught Plato trac'd th' almighty cause,
  And left the wond'ring multitude behind.

Thus ASHLEY gather'd Academic bays ;
  Thus gentle THOMSON, as the Seasons roll,

Taught them to sing the great CREATOR's praise,
  And bear their poet's name from pole to pole.

Thus have I walk'd along the dewy lawn ;
  My frequent foot the blooming wild hath worn ;
Before the lark I 've sung the beauteous dawn,
  And gather'd health from all the gales of morn.

And, even when Winter chill'd the aged year,
  I wander'd lonely o'er the hoary plain ;
Tho' frosty Boreas warn'd me to forbear,
  Boreas, with all its tempests, warn'd in vain.

Then, sleep my nights, and quiet bless'd my days ;
  I fear'd no loss, my MIND was all my store ;
No anxious wishes e'er disturb'd my ease ;
  Heav'n gave content and health—I ask'd no more.

Now Spring returns : but not to me returns
  The vernal joy my better years have known ;
Dim in my breast life's dying taper burns,
  And all the joys of life with health are flown.

Starting and shiv'ring in th' inconstant wind,
  Meagre and pale, the ghost of what I was,
Beneath some blasted tree I lie reclin'd,
  And count the silent moments as they pass :

The winged moments, whose unstaying speed
  No art can stop, or in their course arrest ;
Whose flight shall shortly count me with the dead,
  And lay me down in peace with them that rest.

Oft morning-dreams presage approaching fate ;
  And morning-dreams, as poets tell, are true.
Led by pale ghosts, I enter Death's dark gate,
  And bid the realms of light and life adieu.

I hear the helpless wail, the shriek of wo ;
  I see the muddy wave, the dreary shore,
The sluggish streams that slowly creep below,
  Which mortals visit, and return no more.

Farewell, ye blooming fields ! ye cheerful plains !
  Enough for me the churchyard's lonely mound,
Where Melancholy with still Silence reigns,
  And the rank grass waves o'er the cheerless ground.

There let me wander at the shut of eve,
  When sleep sits dewy on the labourer's eyes,
The world and all its busy follies leave,
  And talk with Wisdom where my DAPHNIS lies.

There let me sleep forgotten in the clay,
  When death shall shut these weary aching eyes,
Rest in the hopes of an eternal day,
  Till the long night's gone, and the last morn arise.

TOMB OF MICHAEL BRUCE, PORTMOAK.

III.

Hymns and Paraphrases.

HYMNS AND PARAPHRASES.[1]

I.[2]   JOB xiv. 1-15.

FEW are thy days and full of woe,
 O man of woman born !
Thy doom is written, dust thou art.
 And shalt to dust return.

Determin'd are the days that fly
 Successive o'er thy head ;
The number'd hour is on the wing,
 That lays thee with the dead.

Alas ! the little day of life
 Is shorter than a span ;
Yet black with thousand hidden ills
 To miserable man.

Gay is thy morning, flattering Hope
 Thy sprightly step attends ;
But soon the tempest howls behind,
 And the dark night descends.

(a) [1] See Writings, p. 39; also Appendix A.   In the following
footnotes : P = Assembly's Translations and Paraphrases. ; L.V. =
Logan's Volume.

[2] P. viii.   L.V., 2, entitled, "The Complaint of Nature."

I

Before its splendid hour the cloud
    Comes o'er the beam of light ;
A Pilgrim in a weary land,
    Man tarries but a night.

Behold ! sad emblem of thy state,
    The flowers that paint the field ;
Or trees, that crown the mountain's brow,
    And boughs and blossoms yield.

When chill the blast of Winter blows,
    Away the Summer flies,
The flowers resign their sunny robes,
    And all their beauty dies.

Nipt by the year the forest fades ;
    And shaking to the wind,
The leaves toss to and fro, and streak
    The wilderness behind.

The Winter past, reviving flowers
    Anew shall paint the plain,
The woods shall hear the voice of Spring,
    And flourish green again.

But man departs this earthly scene,
    Ah ! never to return !
No second Spring shall e'er revive
    The ashes of the urn.

Th' inexorable doors of death
    What hand can e'er unfold ?

Who from the cearments of the tomb
  Can raise the human mold ?

The mighty flood that rolls along
  Its torrents to the main,
The waters lost can ne'er recall
  From that abyss again.

The days, the years, the ages, dark
  Descending down to night,
Can never, never be redeem'd
  Back to the gates of light.

So Man departs the living scene,
  To Night's perpetual gloom ;
The voice of Morning ne'er shall break
  The slumbers of the tomb.

Where are our Fathers ?   Whither gone
  The mighty men of old ?
" The Patriarchs, Prophets, Princes, Kings,
  In sacred books enroll'd.

" Gone to the resting-place of man,
  The everlasting home,
Where ages past have gone before,
  Where future ages come."

Thus Nature pour'd the wail of woe,
  And urged her earnest cry ;
Her voice in agony extreme
  Ascended to the sky.

Th' Almighty heard : then from His throne
 In majesty He rose ;
And from the Heaven, that open'd wide,
 His voice in mercy flows.

" When mortal man resigns his breath,
 And falls a clod of clay,
The soul immortal wings its flight,
 To never-setting day.

" Prepar'd of old for wicked men
 The bed of torment lies ;
The just shall enter into bliss
 Immortal in the skies."

II.[1] Job xxvi. 6 to the end.

WHO can resist th' Almighty arm
 That made the starry sky ?
Or who elude the certain glance
 Of God's all-seeing eye ?

From Him no cov'ring vails our crimes :
 Hell opens to His sight ;
And all Destruction's secret snares
 Lie full disclosed in light.

Firm on the boundless void of space
 He poised the steady pole,
And in the circle of His clouds
 Bade secret waters roll.

<hr>

[1] P. ix.

While nature's universal frame
    Its Maker's power reveals,
His throne, remote from mortal eyes,
    An awful cloud conceals.

From where the rising day ascends,
    To where it sets in night,
He compasses the floods with bounds,
    And checks their threat'ning might.

The pillars that support the sky
    Tremble at His rebuke ;
Through all its caverns quakes the earth,
    As though its centre shook.

He brings the waters from their beds,
    Although no tempest blows,
And smites the kingdom of the proud
    Without the hand of foes.

With bright inhabitants above
    He fills the heav'nly land,
And all the crooked serpent's breed
    Dismay'd before Him stand.

Few of His works can we survey ;
    These few our skill transcend :
But the full thunder of His pow'r
    What heart can comprehend ?

III.[1] PROV. i. 20-31.

In streets, and op'nings of the gates,
  Where pours the busy crowd,
Thus heav'nly Wisdom lifts her voice,
  And cries to men aloud:

How long, ye scorners of the truth,
  Scornful will ye remain?
How long shall fools their folly love,
  And hear my words in vain?

O turn, at last, at my reproof!
  And, in that happy hour,
His bless'd effusions on your heart
  My Spirit down shall pour.

But since so long, with earnest voice,
  To you in vain I call,
Since all my counsels and reproofs
  Thus ineffectual fall;

The time will come, when humbled low,
  In Sorrow's evil day,
Your voice by anguish shall be taught,
  But taught too late, to pray.

When, like the whirlwind, o'er the deep
  Comes Desolation's blast:
Prayers then extorted shall be vain,
  The hour of mercy past.

[1] P. x.

The choice you made has fix'd your doom ;
   For this is Heaven's decree,
That with the fruits of what he sow'd
   The sinner filled shall be.

IV.[1] PROV. iii. 13-17.

O HAPPY is the man who hears
   Instruction's warning voice,
And who celestial Wisdom makes
   His early, only choice.

For she has treasures greater far
   Than East or West unfold,
And her reward is more secure
   Than is the gain of gold.

In her right hand she holds to view
   A length of happy years ;
And in her left, the prize of Fame
   And Honour bright appears.

She guides the young, with innocence,
   In Pleasure's path to tread,
A crown of glory she bestows
   Upon the hoary head.

According as her labours rise,
   So her rewards increase,
Her ways are ways of pleasantness,
   And all her paths are peace.

P. xi. L.V., 4, entitled, "Heavenly Wisdom."

V.[1]   MICAH vi. 6-9.

THUS speaks the heathen : How shall man
  The Power Supreme adore !
With what accepted off'rings come
  His mercy to implore ?

Shall clouds of incense to the skies
  With grateful odour speed ?
Or victims from a thousand hills
  Upon the altar bleed ?

Does justice nobler blood demand
  To save the sinner's life ?
Shall, trembling, in his offspring's side
  The father plunge the knife ?

No : God rejects the bloody rites
  Which blindfold zeal began ;
His oracles of truth proclaim
  The message brought to man.

He what is good hath clearly shown,
  O favour'd race ! to thee ;
And what doth God require of those
  Who bend to Him the knee ?

Thy deeds, let sacred justice rule ;
  Thy heart, let mercy fill ;
And, walking humbly with thy God,
  To Him resign thy will.

[1] P. xxxi.

VI.[1] LUKE ii. 25-33.

WHEN Jesus, by the Virgin brought,
  So runs the law of Heaven,
Was offer'd holy to the Lord,
  And at the altar given :

Simeon the Just and the Devout,
  Who frequent in the fane
Had for the Saviour waited long,
  But waited still in vain ;

Came Heaven-directed at the hour
  When Mary held her son ;
He stretched forth his aged arms,
  While tears of gladness run :

With holy joy upon his face
  The good old father smiled,
While fondly in his wither'd arms
  He clasp'd the promis'd child.

And then he lifted up to Heaven
  An earnest, asking eye ;
My joy is full, my hour is come,
  Lord, let thy servant die.

At last my arms embrace my Lord,
  Now let their vigour cease ;
At last my eyes my Saviour see,
  Now let them close in peace !

[1] L.V., 8. P. xxxviii. (another version).

The star and glory of the land
  Hath now begun to shine ;
The morning that shall gild the globe
  Breaks on these eyes of mine !

VII.[1] 1 THESSAL. iv. 13 to the end.

TAKE comfort, Christians, when your friends
  In Jesus fall asleep ;
Their better being never ends ;
  Why then dejected weep ?

Why inconsolable, as those
  To whom no hope is given ?
Death is the messenger of peace,
  And calls the soul to heaven.

As Jesus died, and rose again
  Victorious from the dead ;
So His disciples rise, and reign
  With their triumphant Head.

The time draws nigh, when from the clouds
  Christ shall with shouts descend,
And the last trumpet's awful voice
  The heav'ns and earth shall rend.

Then they who live shall changed be,
  And they who sleep shall wake ;
The graves shall yield their ancient charge,
  And earth's foundations shake.

            [1] P. liii.

The saints of God, from death set free,
  With joy shall mount on high ;
The heav'nly host, with praises loud,
  Shall meet them in the sky.

Together to their Father's house
  With joyful hearts they go ;
And dwell for ever with the Lord,
  Beyond the reach of woe.

A few short years of evil past,
  We reach the happy shore,
Where death-divided friends at last
  Shall meet to part no more.

VIII.[1] HEB. iv. 14 to the end.

WHERE high the heavenly temple stands,
The house of God not made with hands,
A great High Priest our Nature wears,
The Patron of mankind appears.

He who for men in mercy stood,
And pour'd on earth His precious blood,
Pursues in Heaven His plan of Grace,
The Guardian God of human race.

Tho' now ascended up on high,
He bends on earth a brother's eye,
Partaker of the human name,
He knows the frailty of our frame.

[1] P. lviii.

Our fellow-sufferer yet retains
A fellow-feeling of our pains ;
And still remembers in the skies
His tears, and agonies, and cries.

In every pang that rends the heart,
The Man of Sorrows had a part ;
He sympathises in our grief,
And to the sufferer sends relief.

With boldness, therefore, at the throne
Let us make all our sorrows known,
And ask the aids of heavenly power,
To help us in the evil hour.

IX.[1]

THE hour of my departure's come ;
I hear the voice that calls me home :
At last, O Lord ! let trouble cease,
And let Thy servant die in peace.

The race appointed I have run ;
The combat's o'er, the prize is won ;
And now my witness is on high,
And now my record's in the sky.

Not in mine innocence I trust ;
I bow before Thee in the dust ;
And through my Saviour's blood alone
I look for mercy at thy throne.

[1] Hymn V.   Appended to the Assembly's Collection of Translations
and Paraphrases.

I leave the world without a tear,
Save for the friends I held so dear ;
To heal their sorrows, Lord, descend,
And to the friendless prove a friend.

I come, I come, at Thy command,
I give my spirit to Thy hand ;
Stretch forth Thine everlasting arms,
And shield me in the last alarms.

The hour of my departure 's come :
I hear the voice that calls me home :
Now, O my God ! let trouble cease :
Now let Thy servant die in peace.

X.[1]

ALMIGHTY Father of mankind,
  On Thee my hopes remain ;
And when the day of trouble comes,
  I shall not trust in vain.

Thou art our kind Preserver, from
  The cradle to the tomb ;
And I was cast upon Thy care,
  Even from my mother's womb.

In early years Thou wast my guide,
  And of my youth the friend :
And as my days began with Thee,
  With Thee my days shall end.

[1] L.V., 3, entitled, "Trust in Providence."

I know the Power in whom I trust,
The arm on which I lean ;
He will my Saviour ever be,
Who has my Saviour been.

In former times, when trouble came,
Thou didst not stand afar ;
Nor didst thou prove an absent friend
Amid the din of war.

My God, who causedst me to hope,
When life began to beat,
And when a stranger in the world,
Didst guide my wandering feet :

Thou wilt not cast me off, when age
And evil days descend ;
Thou wilt not leave me in despair,
To mourn my latter end.

Therefore in life I 'll trust to Thee,
In death I will adore ;
And after death will sing thy praise,
When time shall be no more.

XI.[1] Isaiah xlii. 1-13.

Behold ! th' Ambassador divine,
Descending from above,
To publish to mankind the law
Of everlasting love !

[1] P. xviii. (slightly altered.) L. V., 6.

On Him in rich effusion pour'd
    The heavenly dew descends ;
And truth divine He shall reveal,
    To earth's remotest ends.

No trumpet-sound, at His approach,
    Shall strike the wondering ears ;
But still and gentle breathe the voice
    In which the God appears.

By His kind hand the shaken reed
    Shall raise its falling frame ;
The dying embers shall revive,
    And kindle to a flame.

The onward progress of His zeal
    Shall never know decline,
Till foreign lands and distant isles
    Receive the law divine.

He who spread forth the arch of Heaven,
    And bade the planets roll,
Who laid the basis of the earth,
    And form'd the human soul ;

Thus saith the Lord, "Thee have I sent,
    A Prophet from the sky,
Wide o'er the nations to proclaim
    The message from on high.

"Before thy face the shades of death
    Shall take to sudden flight,

The people who in darkness dwell
　　Shall hail a glorious light :

" The gates of brass shall 'sunder burst,
　　The iron fetters fall ;
The promis'd jubilee of Heaven
　　Appointed rise o'er all.

" And lo ! presaging thy approach,
　　The Heathen temples shake,
And trembling in forsaken fanes,
　　The fabled idols quake.

" I am Jehovah : I am One :
　　My name shall now be known ;
No Idol shall usurp my praise,
　　Nor mount into my throne."

Lo, former scenes, predicted once,
　　Conspicuous rise to view ;
And future scenes, predicted now,
　　Shall be accomplish'd too.

Now sing a new song to the Lord !
　　Let earth His praise resound ;
Ye who upon the ocean dwell,
　　And fill the isles around.

O city of the Lord ! begin
　　The universal song ;
And let the scattered villages
　　The joyful notes prolong.

Let Kedar's wilderness afar
  Lift up the lonely voice ;
And let the tenants of the rock
  With accent rude rejoice.

O from the streams of distant lands
  Unto Jehovah sing !
And joyful from the mountain tops
  Shout to the Lord the King ;

Let all combined with one accord
  Jehovah's glories raise,
Till in remotest bounds of earth
  The nations sound His praise.

XII.[1]

MESSIAH ! at Thy glad approach
  The howling wilds are still :
Thy praises fill the lonely waste,
  And breathe from every hill.

The hidden fountains at Thy call
  Their sacred stores unlock ;
Loud in the desert sudden streams
  Burst living from the rock.

The incense of the Spring ascends
  Upon the morning gale ;
Red o'er the hill the roses bloom,
  The lilies in the vale.

[1] L.V., 7.

K

Renew'd, the earth a robe of light,
  A robe of beauty wears ;
And in new heavens a brighter Sun
  Leads on the promised years.

The kingdom of Messiah come,
  Appointed times disclose ;
And fairer in Emmanuel's land
  The new Creation glows.

Let Israel to the Prince of Peace
  The loud Hosannah sing !
With Hallelujahs and with hymns,
  O Zion, hail thy King !

XIII.[1]

BEHOLD ! the mountain of the Lord
  In latter days shall rise,
Above the mountains and the hills,
  And draw the wondering eyes.

To this the joyful nations round
  All tribes and tongues shall flow,
Up to the Hill of God they 'll say,
  And to His house we 'll go.

The beam that shines on Zion hill
  Shall lighten every land ;
The King who reigns in Zion towers
  Shall all the world command.

                    [1] L. V., 5.

No strife shall vex Messiah's reign,
  Or mar the peaceful years :
To ploughshares soon they beat their swords,
  To pruning-hooks their spears.

No longer hosts encountering hosts,
  Their millions slain deplore :
They hang the trumpet in the hall,
  And study war no more.

Come then—O come from every land,
  To worship at His shrine :
And, walking in the light of God,
  With holy beauties shine.

IV.

Miscellaneous Pieces.

WEAVING SPIRITUALIZED.

A WEB I hear thou hast begun,
And know'st not when it may be done—
So death uncertain see ye fear—
For ever distant, ever near.

See'st thou the shuttle quickly pass—
Think mortal life is as the grass,—
An empty cloud—a morning dream—
A bubble rising on the stream.

The knife still ready to cut off
Excrescent knots that mar the stuff,
To stern affliction's rod compare—
'Tis for thy good, so learn to bear.

Too full a quill oft checks the speed
Of shuttle flying by the reed—
So riches oft keep back the soul,
That else would hasten to its goal.

Thine eye the web runs keenly o'er
For things amiss, unseen before,—
Thus scan thy life—mend what's amiss
Next day correct the faults of this.

For when the web is at an end,
'Tis then too late a fault to mend—
Let thought of this awaken dread,—
Repentance dwells not with the dead.

INSCRIPTION ON A BIBLE.

(*f*) 'TIS folly to rejoice and boast
How small a price my Bible cost ;
The day of judgment will make clear
'Twas very cheap—or very dear.

SIR JAMES THE ROSS.

AN HISTORICAL BALLAD.

"I never tried anything which fell in with my inclination so. The Historical Ballad is a species of writing by itself. The common people confound it with the song, but in truth they are widely different. A song should never be historical. It is generally founded on some thought which must be prosecuted and exhibited in every light with a quickness and turn of expression peculiar to itself. The ballad, again, is founded on some passage of history or (what suits its nature better) of tradition. Here the poet may use his liberty, and cut and carve as he has a mind. I think it a kind of writing remarkably adapted to the Scottish Language."—*Extracted from a letter of Michael Bruce to D. Pearson.*

OF all the Scottish northern chiefs,
    Of high and mighty name,
The bravest was Sir James the Ross,
    A knight of meikle fame.

His growth was like a youthful oak
    That crowns the mountain's brow ;
And waving o'er his shoulders broad
    His locks of yellow flew.

Wide were his fields ; his herds were large ;
   And large his flocks of sheep :
And numerous were his goats and deer
   Upon the mountains steep.

The chieftain of the good clan Ross,
   A firm and warlike band :
Five hundred warriors drew the sword
   Beneath his high command.

In bloody fight thrice had he stood
   Against the English keen,
Ere two-and-twenty op'ning springs
   The blooming youth had seen.

The fair Matilda dear he lov'd,
   A maid of beauty rare ;
Even Marg'ret on the Scottish throne
   Was never half so fair.

Long had he woo'd : long she refus'd,
   With seeming scorn and pride ;
Yet oft her eyes confess'd the love
   Her fearful words deny'd.

At length she bless'd his well-try'd love,
   Allow'd his tender claim :
She vow'd to him her virgin heart,
   And own'd an equal flame.

Her father, Buchan's cruel lord,
   Their passion disapprov'd :

He bade her wed Sir John the Græme,
 And leave the youth she lov'd.

One night they met, as they were wont,
 Deep in a shady wood ;
Where on the bank, beside the burn,
 A blooming saugh-tree stood.

Conceal'd among the underwood
 The crafty Donald lay,
The brother of Sir John the Græme,
 To watch what they might say.

When thus the maid began :—"My sire
 Our passion disapproves ;
He bids me wed Sir John the Græme,
 So here must end our loves.

"My father's will must be obey'd,
 Nought boots me to withstand :
Some fairer maid in beauty's bloom
 Shall bless thee with her hand.

"Soon will Matilda be forgot,
 And from thy mind effac'd ;
But may that happiness be thine
 Which I can never taste."

"What do I hear ? Is this thy vow ?"
 Sir James the Ross reply'd :
"And will Matilda wed the Græme,
 Tho' sworn to be my bride ?

His sword shall sooner pierce my heart
   Than reave me of thy charms "—
And clasp'd her to his throbbing breast,
   Fast lock'd within her arms.

"I spoke to try thy love," she said ;
   "I 'll ne'er wed man but thee ;
The grave shall be my bridal bed.
   If Græme my husband be.

"Take then, dear youth ! this faithful kiss,
   In witness of my troth ;
And every plague become my lot,
   That day I break my oath."

They parted thus—the sun was set :
   Up hasty Donald flies ;
And "Turn thee, turn thee, beardless youth ! "
   He loud insulting cries.

Soon turn'd about the fearless chief,
   And soon his sword he drew :
For Donald's blade before his breast
   Had pierc'd his tartans thro'.

"This for my brother's slighted love :
   His wrongs sit on my arm."—
Three paces back the youth retir'd,
   And sav'd himself from harm.

Returning swift, his sword he rear'd
   Fierce Donald's head above :

And thro' the brain and crashing bone
  The furious weapon drove.

Life issued at the wound ; he fell,
  A lump of lifeless clay :
"So fall my foes," quoth valiant Ross,
  And stately strode away.

Thro' the green wood in haste he pass'd
  Unto Lord Buchan's hall :
Beneath Matilda's windows stood,
  And thus on her did call :

"Art thou asleep, Matilda fair ?
  Awake, my love, awake :
Behold thy lover waits without,
  A long farewell to take.

"For I have slain fierce Donald Græme,
  His blood is on my sword :
And far, far distant are my men,
  Nor can defend their lord.

"To Skye I will direct my flight,
  Where my brave brothers bide :
And raise the mighty of the Isles
  To combat on my side."

"O, do not so," the maid replied,
  "With me till morning stay ;
For dark and dreary is the night,
  And dangerous is the way.

" All night I 'll watch thee in the park :
　My faithful page I 'll send
In haste to raise the brave clan Ross,
　Their master to defend."

He laid him down beneath a bush,
　And wrapt him in his plaid ;
While, trembling for her lover's fate,
　At distance stood the maid.

Swift ran the page o'er hill and dale ;
　Till, in a lowly glen,
He met the furious Sir John Græme,
　With twenty of his men.

" Where go'st ? thou, little page !" he said :
　So late who did thee send ?"
" I go to raise the brave clan Ross,
　Their master to defend.

" For he has slain fierce Donald Græme,
　His blood is on his sword ;
And far, far distant are his men,
　Nor can assist their lord."

" And has he slain my brother dear ?"
　The furious chief replies :
" Dishonour blast my name ! but he
　By me, ere morning, dies.

" Say, page ! where is Sir James the Ross ?
　I will thee well reward."

" He sleeps into Lord Buchan's park ;
    Matilda is his guard."

They spurr'd their steeds, and furious flew,
    Like lightning, o'er the lea :
They reach'd Lord Buchan's lofty tow'rs
    By dawning of the day.

Matilda stood without the gate,
    Upon a rising ground,
And watched each object in the dawn,
    All ear to every sound.

" Where sleeps the Ross ?" began the Græme,
    "Or has the felon fled ?
This hand shall lay the wretch on earth,
    By whom my brother bled."

And now the valiant knight awoke,
    The Virgin shrieking heard :
Straight up he rose, and drew his sword,
    When the fierce band appear'd.

" Your sword last night my brother slew,
    His blood yet dims its shine ;
And, ere the sun shall gild the morn,
    Your blood shall reek on mine."

" Your words are brave," the chief return'd,
    "But deeds approve the man :
Set by your men, and hand to hand
    We'll try what valour can."

With dauntless step he forward strode,
  And dar'd him to the fight :
The Græme gave back and fear'd his arm,
  For well he knew his might.

Four of his men, the bravest four,
  Sunk down beneath his sword ;
But still he scorn'd the poor revenge,
  And sought their haughty lord.

Behind him basely came the Græme,
  And pierc'd him in the side :
Out spouting came the purple stream,
  And all his tartans dy'd.

But yet his hand not dropped the sword,
  Nor sunk he to the ground,
Till thro' his en'my's heart his steel
  Had forc'd a mortal wound.

Græme, like a tree by winds o'erthrown,
  Fell breathless on the clay ;
And down beside him sunk the Ross,
  And faint and dying lay.

Matilda saw, and fast she ran :
  "O spare his life," she cried :
Lord Buchan's daughter begs his life,
  Let her not be denied.

Her well-known voice the hero heard ;
  He rais'd his death-closed eyes ;

He fix'd them on the weeping maid,
　And weakly thus replies :

" In vain Matilda begs the life
　　By death's arrest deny'd ;
My race is run—Adieu, my love ! "
　　Then clos'd his eyes and dy'd.

The sword yet warm, from his left side
　With frantic hand she drew :
" I come, Sir James the Ross," she cried,
　" I come to follow you."

The hilt she lean'd against the ground,
　And bar'd her snowy breast ;
Then fell upon her lover's face,
　And sunk to endless rest.

ODE:

TO A FOUNTAIN.

O FOUNTAIN of the wood ! whose glassy wave,
　Slow-welling from the rock of years,
　　Holds to heav'n a mirror blue,
　　And bright as Anna's eye,

With whom I 've sported on the margin green :
　My hand with leaves, with lilies white,
　　Gaily deck'd her golden hair,
　　Young Naiad of the vale.

Fount of my native wood ! thy murmurs greet
　My ear, like poet's heavenly strain :

Fancy pictures in a dream
The golden days of youth.

O state of innocence ! O paradise !
In Hope's gay garden, Fancy views
Golden blossoms, golden fruits,
And Eden ever green.

Where now, ye dear companions of my youth !
Ye brothers of my bosom ! where
Do ye tread the walks of life,
Wide scatter'd o'er the world ?

Thus wingéd larks forsake their native nest,
The merry minstrels of the morn :
New to heav'n they mount away,
And meet again no more.

All things decay : the forest like the leaf :
Great kingdoms fall ; the peopled globe,
Planet-struck, shall pass away :
Heav'ns with their hosts expire :

But Hope's fair visions, and the beams of Joy,
Shall cheer my bosom : I will sing
Nature's beauty, Nature's birth.
And heroes on the lyre.

Ye Naiads ! blue-eyed sisters of the wood !
Who by old oak, or storied stream,
Nightly tread your mystic maze,
And charm the wand'ring Moon,

L

Beheld by poet's eye ; inspire my dreams
With visions, like the landscapes fair
  Of heav'n's bliss, to dying saints
    By guardian angels drawn.

Fount of the forest ! in thy poet's lays
Thy waves shall flow : this wreath of flow'rs,
  Gather'd by my Anna's hand,
    I ask to bind my brow.

DANISH ODE.

The great, the glorious deed is done!
The foe is fled ! the field is won !
Prepare the feast, the heroes call ;
Let joy, let triumph fill the hall !

The raven claps his sable wings ;
The Bard his chosen timbrel brings :
Six virgins round, a select choir,
Sing to the music of his lyre.

With mighty ale the goblet crown ;
With mighty ale your sorrows drown :
To-day, to mirth and joy we yield ;
To-morrow, face the bloody field.

From danger's front, at battle's eve,
Sweet comes the banquet to the brave :
Joy shines with genial beam on all,
The joy that dwells in Odin's hall.

The song bursts living from the lyre,
Like dreams that guardian ghosts inspire :
When mimic shrieks the heroes hear,
And whirl the visionary spear.

Music 's the med'cine of the mind ;
The cloud of Care give to the wind ;
Be ev'ry brow with garlands bound,
And let the cup of Joy go round.

The cloud comes o'er the beam of light ;
We 're guests that tarry but a night :
In the dark house, together press'd,
The princes and the people rest.

Send round the shell, the feast prolong,
And send away the night in song ;
Be blest below, as those above
With Odin's and the friends they love.

DANISH ODE.

In deeds of arms, our fathers rise,
Illustrious in their offspring's eyes :
They fearless rush'd through Ocean's storms,
And dar'd grim Death in all its forms ;
Each youth assum'd the sword and shield,
And grew a hero in the field.

Shall we degenerate from our race,
Inglorious, in the mountain chase ?
Arm, arm in fallen Hubba's right ;

Place your forefathers in your sight;
To fame, to glory fight your way,
And teach the nations to obey.

Assume the oars, unbind the sails;
Send, Odin! send propitious gales.
At Loda's stone, we will adore
Thy name with songs, upon the shore:
And, full of thee, undaunted dare
The foe, and dart the bolts of war.

No feast of shells, no dance by night,
Are glorious Odin's dear delight:
He, king of men, his armies led,
Where heroes strove, where battles bled;
Now reigns above the morning-star,
The god of thunder and of war.

Bless'd who in battle bravely fall!
They mount on wings to Odin's Hall;
To Music's sound, in cups of gold,   .
They drink new wine with chiefs of old;
The song of bards records their name,
And future times shall speak their fame.

Hark! Odin thunders! haste on board;
Illustrious Canute! give the word.
On wings of wind we pass the seas,
To conquer realms, if Odin please:
With Odin's spirit in our soul,
We'll gain the globe from pole to pole.

TO PAOLI.

Dr R. Small, in the *British and Foreign Evangelical Review*, says that he can show that "the materials for such an Ode were not in existence until a twelvemonth after Bruce's death. Bruce died in 1767. Corsica was sold to the French in the following year, and then came the tug-of-war." So Mr Small; and he infers from this that the Ode to Paoli could not have been written earlier than 1768, and, therefore, not by Bruce.

But "the tug-of-war" between Corsica and her enemies, under the leadership of Paoli, began not in 1768, but in 1755, the year in which he was invited by the Corsicans to become generalissimo, and the point from which his earliest and noblest efforts on behalf of his countrymen commence. Paoli gained decisive victories over the Genoese before their surrender of the island to the French in 1768. The lines "Whose firm resolve obeys a nation's call" fitly apply to the invitation to Paoli in 1755, and the thousands marching in his rear are explained by the poet's vision of the gathering of the people who had called him to their aid.

WHAT man, what hero shall the Muses sing,
On classic lyre or Caledonian string ?
 Whose name shall fill th' immortal page ?
Who, fir'd from heav'n with energy divine,
In sun-bright glory bids his actions shine
 First in the annals of the age ?
 Ceas'd are the golden times of yore ;
 The age of heroes is no more :
Rare, in these latter times, arise to fame
The poet's strain inspir'd, or hero's heav'nly flame.

What star arising in the southern sky,
New to the heav'ns, attracting Europe's eye,
 With beams unborrow'd shines afar ?
Who comes, with thousands marching in his rear,
Shining in arms, shaking his bloody spear,
 Like the red comet, sign of war ?

Paoli ! sent of Heav'n, to save
A rising nation of the brave ;
Whose firm right hand his angels arm, to bear
A shield before his host, and dart the bolts of war.

He comes ! he comes ! the saviour of the land '
His drawn sword flames in his uplifted hand,
    Enthusiast in his country's cause ;
Whose firm resolve obeys a nation's call,
To rise deliverer, or a martyr fall
    To Liberty, to dying laws.
  Ye sons of Freedom ! sing his praise ;
  Ye poets ! bind his brows with bays ;
Ye sceptr'd shadows ! cast your honours down,
And bow before the head that never wore a crown.

Who to the hero can the palm refuse ?
Great Alexander still the world subdues,
    The heir of everlasting praise.
But when the hero's flame, the patriot's light ;
When virtues human and divine unite ;
    When olives twine among the bays,
  And, mutual, both Minervas shine ;
  A constellation so divine,
A wond'ring world behold, admire, and love.
And his best image here, th' Almighty marks above.

As the lone shepherd hides him in the rocks,
When high heav'n thunders ; as the tim'rous flocks
    From the descending torrent flee :
So flies a world of Slaves at War's alarms,
When Zeal on flame, and Liberty in arms,

Leads on the fearless and the free,
Resistless ; as the torrent flood,
Horn'd like the moon, uproots the wood,
Sweeps flocks, and herds, and harvests from their base,
And moves th' eternal hills from their appointed place.

Long hast thou labour'd in the glorious strife,
O land of Liberty ! profuse of life,
    And prodigal of priceless blood.
Where heroes bought with blood the martyr's crown,
A race arose, heirs of their high renown,
    Who dar'd their fate thro' fire and flood :
    And Gaffori the great arose,
    Whose words of pow'r disarm'd his foes ;
And where the filial image smil'd afar,
The sire turned not aside the thunders of the war.

O Liberty ! to man a guardian giv'n,
Thou best and brightest attribute of Heav'n !
    From whom descending, thee we sing.
By nature wild, or by the arts refin'd,
We feel thy pow'r essential to our mind ;
    Each son of Freedom is a king.
    Thy praise the happy world proclaim,
    And Britain worships at thy name,
Thou guardian angel of Britannia's isle !
And God and man rejoice in thy immortal smile !

Island of beauty ! lift thy head on high ;
Sing a new son of triumph to the sky !
    The day of thy deliv'rance springs !
The day of vengeance to thy ancient foe.

Thy sons shall lay the proud oppressor low,
  And break the head of tyrant kings.
 Paoli! mighty man of war!
 All bright in arms, thy conqu'ring car
Ascend; thy people from the foe redeem,
Thou delegate of Heav'n, and son of the Supreme!

Ruled by th' eternal laws, supreme o'er all,
Kingdoms, like kings, successive rise and fall.
  When Cæsar conquer'd half the earth,
And spread his eagles in Britannia's sun,
Did Cæsar dream the savage huts he won
   Should give a far-famed kingdom birth?
  That here should Roman freedom 'light;
  The western Muses wing their flight;
The Arts, the Graces find their fav'rite home;
Our armies awe the globe, and Britain rival Rome?

Thus, if th' Almighty say, "Let Freedom be,"
Thou Corsica! thy golden age shalt see.
  Rejoice with songs, rejoice with smiles;
Worlds yet unfound, and ages yet unborn,
Shall hail a new Britannia in her morn,
   The Queen of arts, the Queen of isles:
  The Arts, the beauteous train of Peace,
  Shall rise and rival Rome and Greece;
A Newton Nature's book unfold sublime:
A Milton sing to Heav'n, and charm the ear of Time!

THE EAGLE, CROW, AND SHEPHERD.

A FABLE.

BENEATH the horror of a rock,
A shepherd careless fed his flock.
Souse from its top an eagle came,
And seiz'd upon a sporting lamb;
Its tender sides his talons tear,
And bear it bleating thro' the air.

This was discover'd by a crow,
Who hopp'd upon the plain below.
" Yon ram," says he, " becomes my prey " :
And, mounting, hastens to the fray,
Lights on his back—when lo, ill-luck !
He in the fleece entangled stuck ;
He spreads his wings, but can't get free,
Struggling in vain for liberty.

The shepherd soon the captive spies,
And soon he seizes on the prize.
His children curious crowd around,
And ask what strange fowl he has found ?
" My sons," said he, " warn'd by this wretch,
Attempt no deed above your reach :
An eagle not an hour ago,
He 's now content to be a crow."

THE MUSIAD: A MINOR EPIC POEM.

IN THE MANNER OF HOMER.   A FRAGMENT.

IN ancient times, ere traps were fram'd,
  Or cats in Britain's isle were known ;
A mouse, for pow'r and valour fam'd,
  Possess'd in peace the regal throne.

A farmer's house he nightly storm'd,
  (In vain were bolts, in vain were keys ;)
The milk's fair surface he deform'd,
  And digg'd entrenchments in the cheese.

In vain the farmer watch'd by night,
  In vain he spread the poison'd bacon ;
The mouse was wise as well as wight,
  Nor could by force or fraud be taken.

His subjects follow'd where he led,
  And dealt destruction all around ;
His people, shepherd-like, he fed ;
  Such mice are rarely to be found !

But evil fortune had decreed,
  (The foe of mice as well as men,)
The royal mouse at last should bleed,
  Should fall—ne'er to arise again.

Upon a night, as authors say,
  A luckless scent our hero drew,
Upon forbidden ground to stray,
  And pass a narrow cranny through.

That night a feast the farmer made,
   And joy unbounded fill'd the house ;
The fragments in the pantry spread
   Afforded business to the mouse.

He ate his fill, and back again
   Return'd ; but access was deny'd.
He search'd each corner, but in vain ;
   He found it close on every side.

Let none our hero's fears deride ;
   He roar'd (ten mice of modern days,
As mice are dwindl'd and decay'd,
   So great a voice could scarcely raise).

Rous'd at the voice, the farmer ran,
   And seiz'd upon his hapless prey.
With entreaties the mouse began,
   And pray'rs, his anger to allay.

"O spare my life," he trembling cries ;
   "My subjects will a ransom give,
Large as thy wishes can devise,
   Soon as it shall be heard I live."

"No, wretch !" the farmer says in wrath,
   "Thou dy'st ; no ransom I 'll receive."
"My subjects will revenge my death,"
   He said ; "this dying charge I leave."

The farmer lifts his armed hand,
   And on the mouse inflicts a wound.

What mouse could such a blow withstand ?
He fell, and dying bit the ground.

Thus Lambris fell, who flourish'd long,
 (I half forgot to tell his name ;)
But his renown lives in the song,
 And future times shall speak his fame.

A mouse, who walk'd about at large
 In safety, heard his mournful cries ;
He heard him give his dying charge,
 And to the rest he frantic flies.

Thrice he essay'd to speak, and thrice
 Tears, such as mice may shed, fell down.
" Revenge your monarch's death," he cries,
 His voice half-stifl'd with a groan.

But having re-assum'd his senses,
 And reason, such as mice may have,
He told out all the circumstances
 With many a strain and broken heave.

Chill'd with sad grief, th' assembly heard ;
 Each dropp'd a tear, and bow'd the head :
But symptoms soon of rage appear'd,
 And vengeance for their royal dead.

Long sat they mute : at last up rose
 The great Hypenor, blameless sage !
A hero born to many woes ;
 His head was silver'd o'er with age.

His bulk so large, his joints so strong,
  Though worn with grief, and past his prime,
Few rats could equal him, 'tis sung,
  As rats are in these dregs of time.

Two sons, in battle brave, he had,
  Sprung from fair Lalage's embrace ;
Short time they grac'd his nuptial bed,
  By dogs destroy'd in cruel chase.

Their timeless fate the mother wail'd,
  And pined with heart-corroding grief :
O'er every comfort it prevail'd,
  Till death advancing brought relief.

Now he 's the last of all his race,
  A prey to wo : he inly pin'd ;
Grief pictur'd sat upon his face :
  Upon his breast his head reclin'd.

And, "O my fellow-mice !" he said,
  "These eyes ne'er saw a day so dire,
Save when my gallant children bled.
  O wretched sons ! O wretched sire !

" But now a gen'ral cause demands
  Our grief, and claims our tears alone ;
Our monarch, slain by wicked hands,
  No issue left to fill the throne.

" Yet, tho' by hostile man much wrong'd,
  My counsel is, from arms forbear,
That so your days may be prolong'd ;
  For man is Heav'n's peculiar care."

ANACREONTIC : TO A WASP.

The following is a ludicrous imitation of the usual Anacreontics : the spirit of composing which was raging, a few years ago, among all the sweet singers of Great Britain.

WINGÈD wand'rer of the sky !
Inhabitant of heav'n high !
Dreadful with thy dragon tail,
Hydra-head, and coat of mail !
Why dost thou my peace molest ?
Why dost thou disturb my rest ?
When in May the meads are seen,
Sweet enamel ! white and green ;
And the gardens, and the bow'rs,
And the forests, and the flow'rs,
Don their robes of curious dye,
Fine confusion to the eye !
Did I —— chase thee in thy flight ?
Did I ——- put thee in a fright ?
Did I —— spoil thy treasure hid ?
Never—never—never—did.
Envious nothing ! pray beware ;
Tempt mine anger, if you dare.
Trust not in thy strength of wing ;
Trust not in thy length of sting.
Heav'n nor earth shall thee defend ;
I thy buzzing soon will end.
Take my counsel, while you may ;
Devil take you, if you stay.
Wilt—thou—dare—my—face—to—wound ?—
Thus, I fell thee to the ground.
Down amongst the dead men, now

Thou shalt forget thou ere wast thou.
Anacreontic Bards beneath,
Thus shall wail thee after death.

CHORUS OF ELYSIAN BARDS.

" A Wasp, for a wonder,
　To paradise under
　Descends ; See ! he wanders
　By Styx's meanders !
　Behold how he glows,
　Amidst Rhodope's snows
　He sweats, in a trice,
　In the regions of ice !
　Lo ! he cools, by God's ire,
　Amidst brimstone and fire !
　He goes to our king,
　And he shows him his sting.
　(God Pluto loves satire,
　As women love attire ;)
　Our king sets him free,
　Like fam'd Euridice.
　Thus a wasp could prevail
　O'er the Devil and hell,
A conquest both hard and laborious !
　Tho' hell had fast bound him,
　And the Devil did confound him,
Yet his sting and his wing were victorious."

ALEXIS.

A PASTORAL.

Upon a bank with cowslips cover'd o'er,
Where Leven's waters break against the shore ;
What time the village sires in circles talk,
And youths and maidens take their evening walk ;
Among the yellow bloom Alexis lay,
And view'd the beauties of the setting day.

Full well you might observe some inward smart,
Some secret grief hung heavy at his heart.
While round the field his sportive lambkins play'd,
He rais'd his plaintive voice, and thus he said :

Begin, my pipe ! a softly mournful strain.
The parting sun shines yellow on the plain ;
The balmy west-wind breathes along the ground ;
Their evening sweets the flow'rs dispense around ;
The flocks stray bleating o'er the mountain's brow,
And from the plain the answ'ring cattle low :
Sweet chant the feather'd tribes on every tree,
And all things feel the joys of love, but me.

Begin, my pipe ! begin the mournful strain.
Eumelia meets my kindness with disdain.
Oft have I tried her stubborn heart to move,
And in her icy bosom kindle love :
But all in vain—ere I my love declar'd,
With other youths her company I shar'd ;
But now she shuns me hopeless and forlorn,
And pays my constant passion with her scorn.

Begin, my pipe ! the sadly-soothing strain,
And bring the days of innocence again.
Well I remember, in the sunny scene
We ran, we play'd together on the green.
Fair in our youth, and wanton in our play,
We toy'd, we sported the long summer's day.
For her I spoil'd the gardens of the Spring,
And taught the goldfinch on her hand to sing.
We sat and sung beneath the lover's tree :
One was her look, and it was fix'd on me.

Begin, my pipe ! a melancholy strain.
A holiday was kept on yonder plain ;
The feast was spread upon the flow'ry mead,
And skilful Thyrsis tun'd his vocal reed ;
Each for the dance selects the nymph he loves,
And every nymph with smiles her swain approves :
The setting sun beheld their mirthful glee,
And left all happy in their love, but me.

Begin, my pipe ! a softly mournful strain.
O cruel nymph ! O most unhappy swain !
To climb the steepy rock's tremendous height,
And crop its herbage is the goat's delight ;
The flowery thyme delights the humming bees,
The blooming wilds the bleating lambkins please :
Daphnis courts Chloe under every tree :
Eumelia ! you alone have joys for me !

Now cease, my pipe ! now cease the mournful strain.
Lo, yonder comes Eumelia o'er the plain !
Till she approach, I'll lurk behind the shade,
M

Then try with all my art the stubborn maid :
Though to her lover cruel and unkind,
Yet time may change the purpose of her mind.
But vain these pleasing hopes ! already see,
She hath observ'd, and now she flies from me !

Then cease, my pipe ! the unavailing strain.
Apollo aids, the Nine inspire in vain :
You, cruel maid ! refuse to lend an ear ;
No more I sing, since you disdain to hear.
This pipe Amyntas gave, on which he play'd :
" Be thou its second lord," the dying shepherd said.
No more I pray, now silent let it be ;
Nor pipe, nor song, can e'er give joy to me.

DAMON, MENALCAS, AND MELIBŒUS.

AN ECLOGUE.

DAMON.

MILD from the shower, the morning's rosy light
Unfolds the beauteous season to the sight :
The landscape rises verdant on the view ;
The little hills uplift their heads in dew ;
The sunny stream rejoices in the vale ;
The woods with songs approaching summer hail :
The boy comes forth among the flow'rs to play ;
His fair hair glitters in the yellow ray.
Shepherds, begin the song ! while, o'er the mead,
Your flocks at will on dewy pastures feed.
Behold fair nature, and begin the song ;
The songs of nature to the swain belong,
Who equals Cona's bard in sylvan strains,

To him his harp an equal prize remains ;
His harp, which sounds on all its sacred strings
The loves of hunters, and the wars of kings.

MENALCAS.

Now fleecy clouds in clearer skies are seen ;
The air is genial, and the earth is green :
O'er hill and dale the flow'rs spontaneous spring,
And blackbirds singing now invite to sing.

MELIBŒUS.

Now milky show'rs rejoice the springing grain ;
New-opening pea-blooms purple all the plain ;
The hedges blossom white on every hand ;
Already harvest seems to clothe the land.

MENALCAS.

White o'er the hill my snowy sheep appear,
Each with her lamb ; their shepherd's name they bear.
I love to lead them where the daisy spring,
And on the sunny hill to sit and sing.

MELIBŒUS.

My fields are green with clover and with corn ;
My flocks the hills, and herds the vales adorn.
I teach the stream, I teach the vocal shore,
And woods to echo that "I want no more."

MENALCAS.

To me the bees their annual nectar yield ;
Peace cheers my hut, and plenty clothes my field.
I fear no loss : I give to Ocean's wind
All care away, a monarch in my mind.

MELIBŒUS.

My mind is cheerful as the linnet's lays ;
Heav'n daily hears a shepherd's simple praise.
What time I shear my flock, I send a fleece
To aged Mopsa, and her orphan niece.

MENALCAS.

Lavinia, come ! her primroses upspring ;
Here choirs of linnets, here yourself may sing ;
Here meadows worthy of thy foot appear :
O come, Lavinia ! let us wander here !

MELIBŒUS.

Rosella, come ! here flow'rs the heath adorn ;
Here ruddy roses open on the thorn ;
Here willows by the brook a shadow give ;
O here, Rosella ! let us love to live !

MENALCAS.

Lavinia 's fairer than the flow'rs of May,
Or Autumn apples ruddy in the ray :
For her my flow'rs are in a garland wove,
And all my apples ripen for my love.

MELIBŒUS.

Prince of the wood, the oak majestic tow'rs ;
The lily of the vale is queen of flow'rs :
Above the maids Rosella's charms prevail,
As oaks in woods, and lilies in the vale !

MENALCAS.

Resound, ye rocks ! ye little hills ! rejoice !
Assenting woods ! to Heaven uplift your voice !

Let Spring and Summer enter hand in hand ;
Lavinia comes, the glory of our land !

MELIBŒUS.

Whene'er my love appears upon the plain,
To her the wond'ring shepherds tune the strain :
" Who comes in beauty like the vernal morn,
When yellow robes of light all heaven and earth adorn."

MENALCAS.

Rosella 's mine, by all the Pow'rs above ;
Each star in heav'n is witness to our love.
Among the lilies she abides all day ;
Herself as lovely, and as sweet as they.

MELIBŒUS.

By Tweed Lavinia feeds her fleecy care,
And in the sunshine combs her yellow hair.
Be thine the peace of Heav'n, unknown to kings,
And o'er thee angels spread their guardian wings !

MENALCAS.

I followed Nature, and was fond of praise ;
Thrice noble Varo has approved my lays ;
If he approves, superior to my peers,
I join th' immortal choir, and sing to other years.

MELIBŒUS.

My mistress is my Muse : the banks of Tyne
Resound with Nature's music, and with mine ;
Helen the fair, the beauty of our green,
To me adjudg'd the prize when chosen queen.

DAMON.

Now cease your songs : the flocks to shelter fly,
And the high sun has gain'd the middle sky.
To both alike the poet's bays belong,
Chiefs of the choir, and masters of the song.
Thus let your pipes contend, with rival strife,
To sing the praises of the pastoral life :
Sing Nature's scenes with Nature's beauties fir'd ;
Where poets dream'd, where prophets lay inspir'd.
Even Caledonian queens have trod the meads,
And sceptr'd kings assum'd the shepherd's weeds :
Th' angelic choirs, that guard the throne of God,
Have sat with shepherds on the humble sod.
With us renew'd the golden times remain,
And long-lost innocence is found again.

PHILOCLES :

AN ELEGY, ON THE DEATH OF MR WILLIAM DRYBURGH.

WAILING, I sit on Leven's sandy shore,
    And sadly tune the reed to sounds of woe ;
Once more I call Melpomene ! once more
    Spontaneous teach the weeping verse to flow !

The weeping verse shall flow in friendship's name,
    Which friendship asks, and friendship fain would pay ;
The weeping verse, which worth and genius claim.
    Begin then, Muse ! begin thy mournful lay.

Aided by thee, I 'll twine a rustic wreath
    Of fairest flow'rs, to deck the grass-grown grave
Of Philocles, cold in the bed of death,
    And mourn the gentle youth I could not save.

Where lordly Forth divides the fertile plains,
　With ample sweep, a sea from side to side,
A rocky bound his raging course restrains,
　For ever lashed by the resounding tide.

There stands his tomb upon the sea-beat shore,
　Afar discerned by the rough sailor's eye,
Who, passing, weeps, and stops the sounding oar,
　And points where piety and virtue lie.

Like the gay palm on Rabbah's fair domains,
　Or cedar shadowing Carmel's flowery side :
Or, like the upright ash on Britain's plains,
　Which waves its stately arms in youthful pride :

So flourished Philocles : and as the hand
　Of ruthless woodman lays their honours low,
He fell in youth's fair bloom by fate's command,
　'Twas fate that struck, 'tis ours to mourn the blow.

Alas ! we fondly thought that Heaven designed
　His bright example mankind to improve :
All they should be, was pictured in his mind ;
　His thoughts were virtue, and his heart was love.

Calm as a summer's sun's unruffled face,
　He looked unmoved on life's precarious game,
And smiled at mortals toiling in the chase
　Of empty phantoms—opulence and fame.

Steady he followed Virtue's onward path,
　Inflexible to Error's devious way ;

And firm at last, in hope and fixéd faith,
  Thro' Death's dark vale he trod without dismay.

The gloomy vale he trod, relentless Death !
  Where waste and horrid desolation reign.
The tyrant, humbled, there resigns his wrath ;
  The wretch, elated, there forgets his pain :

There sleep the infant, and the hoary head ;
  Together lie the oppressor and the oppressed ;
There dwells the captive, free among the dead :
  There Philocles, and there the weary rest.

The curtains of the grave fast drawn around,
  'Till the loud trumpet wakes the sleep of death,
With dreadful clangour through the world resound,
  Shake the firm globe, and burst the vaults beneath.

Then Philocles shall rise, to glory rise,
  And his Redeemer for himself shall see ;
With Him in triumph mount the azure skies :
  For where He is, His followers shall be.

Whence then these sighs ? and whence this falling tear ?
  To sad remembrance of his merit just,
Still must I mourn, for he to me was dear,
  And still is dear, though buried in the dust.

DAPHNIS: A MONODY.

*To the Memory of Mr William Arnot, son of Mr David Arnot,
of Portmoak, near Kinross.*

[1] "Gairney Bridge, May 29, 1765.—Walking lately by the churchyard of your town, which inspires a kind of veneration for our ancestors, I was struck with these beautiful lines of Mr Gray, in his 'Elegy written in a Country Churchyard':

> ' Perhaps in this neglected spot is laid,
> Some heart once pregnant with celestial fire ';

and immediately I called to mind your son, whose memory will be ever dear unto me ; and, with respect to that place, put the supposition out of doubt. I wrote the most part of that poem the same day, which I should be sorry if you look upon as a piece of flattery : I know you are above flattery, and if I know my own mind, I am so too. It is the language of the heart; I think a lie in prose and verse the same. The versification is irregular, in imitation of Milton's Lycidas."—*Letter from Bruce to Mr David Arnot.*

No more of youthful joys, or love's fond dreams ;
No more of morning fair, or ev'ning mild ;
While Daphnis lies among the silent dead
Unsung ; though long ago he trode the path,
To dreary road of death,
Which soon or late each human foot must tread.
He trod the dark uncomfortable wild
By Faith's pure light, by Hope's heav'n-opening beams ;
By Love, whose image gladdens mortal eyes,
And keeps the golden key that opens all the skies.

Assist, ye Muses !—and ye will assist ;
For Daphnis, whom I sing, to you was dear :
Ye loved the boy, and on his youthful head

[1] Dr MacKelvie, p. 24.

Your kindest influence shed.—
So may I match his lays, who to the lyre
Wailed his lost Lycidas by wood and rill :
So may the Muse my grov'ling mind inspire
To sing a farewell to thy ashes blest ;
To bid fair peace be to thy gentle shade ;
To scatter flowerets, cropt by Fancy's hand,
In sad assemblage round thy tomb,
If watered by the Muse, to latest time to bloom.

Oft by the side of Leven's crystal Lake,
Trembling beneath the closing lids of light,
With slow short-measured steps we took our walk :
Then he would talk
Of argument, far, far above his years ;
Then he would reason high ;
Till from the east the silver Queen of Night
Her journey up heaven's steep began to make,
And Silence reigned attentive in the sky.

O happy days !—for ever, ever gone !
When o'er the flow'ry green we ran, we play'd
With blooms bedropt by youthful Summer's hand :
Or, in the willow's shade,
We mimic castles built among the sand,
Soon by the sounding surge to be beat down,
Or sweeping winds ; when, by the sedgy marsh,
We heard the heron and the wild duck harsh,
And sweeter lark tune his melodious lay,
At highest noon of day.
Among the antic moss-grown stones we 'd roam,
With ancient hieroglyphic figures graced ;

Winged hour-glasses, bones, and skulls, and spades,
And obsolete inscriptions, by the hands
Of other ages. Ah! I little thought
That we then played o'er his untimely tomb.

Where were ye, Muses! when the leaden hand
Of Death, remorseless, clos'd your Daphnis' eyes?
For sure ye heard the weeping mother's cries : —
But the dread pow'r of Fate what can withstand?
Young Daphnis smil'd at Death ; the tyrant's darts
As stubble counted. What was his support?
His conscience, and firm trust in Him whose ways
Are truth ; in Him who sways
His potent sceptre o'er the dark domains
Of death and hell ; who holds in strait'ned reins
Their banded legions ; "Thro' the darksome vale
He'll guide my trembling steps with heavenly ray ;
I see the dawning of immortal day" :
He, smiling, said, and died !—

Hail, and farewell, blest youth! Soon hast thou left
This evil world. Fair was thy thread of life :
But quickly by the envious Sisters shorn.
Thus have I seen a rose with rising morn
Unfold its glowing bloom, sweet to the smell.
And lovely to the eye ; when a keen wind
Hath torn its blushing leaves, and laid it low.
Stripp'd of its sweets. Ah! so,
So Daphnis fell! long ere his prime he fell!
Nor left he on these plains his peer behind ;
These plains, that mourn their loss, of him bereft,
No more look gay, but desert and forlorn.

Now cease your lamentations, shepherds, cease :
Though Daphnis died below, he lives above ;
A better life, and in a fairer clime,
He lives. No sorrow enters that blest place ;
But ceaseless songs of love and joy resound :
And fragrance floats around,
By fanning zephyrs from the spicy groves,
And flowers immortal wafted ; asphodel
And amaranth, unfading, deck the ground,
With fairer colours than, ere Adam fell,
In Eden bloomed. There, haply he may hear
This artless song. Ye powers of verse ! improve,
And make it worthy of your darling's ear,
And make it equal to the shepherd's love.

Thus, in the shadow of a frowning rock,
Beneath a mountain's side, shaggy and hoar,
A homely swain, tending his little flock,
Rude, yet a lover of the Muse's lore,
Chanted his Doric strain till close of day ;
Then rose, and homeward slowly bent his way.

VERSES

ON THE DEATH OF THE REV. WM. M'EWEN.

M'Ewen gone ! and shall the mournful Muse
A tear unto his memory refuse ?
Forbid it, all ye powers that guard the just,
Your care his actions, and his life your trust.
The righteous perish ! is M'Ewen dead ?
In him Religion, Virtue's friend, is fled.

Modest in strife, bold in religion's cause,
He sought true honour in his God's applause.
What manly beauties in his works appear!
Close without straining, and concise though clear.
Though short his life, not so his deathless fame,
Succeeding ages shall revere his name.
Hail, blest immortal, hail! while we are tost,
Thy happy soul is landed on the coast,
That land of bliss, where on the peaceful shore
Thou view'st with pleasure, all thy dangers o'er :
Laid in the silent grave, thy honour'd dust
Expects the resurrection of the just.

TO JOHN MILLAR, M.D.

On recovery from a dangerous fit of illness—(written in the name
of Mr David Pearson).

A RUSTIC youth (he seeks no better name)
Alike unknown to fortune and to fame,
Acknowledging a debt he ne'er can pay,
For thee, O Millar ! frames the artless lay :
That yet he lives, that vital warmth remains,
And life's red tide bounds briskly thro' his veins :
To thee he owes. His grateful heart believe,
And take his thanks sincere, 'tis all he has to give.
Let traders brave the flood in thirst of gain,
Kept with disquietude as got with pain ;
Let heroes, tempted by a sounding name,
Pursue bright honour in the fields of fame.
Can wealth or fame a moment's ease command
To him, who sinks beneath affliction's hand ?
Upon the wither'd limbs fresh beauty shed ;
Or cheer the dark, dark mansions of the dead ?

AN EPIGRAM.

WITH Celia talking, Pray, says I,
    Think you, you could a husband want,
Or would you rather choose to die
    If Heav'n the blessing should not grant ?

Awhile the beauteous maid look'd down,
    Then with a blush she thus began :
" Life is a precious thing I own,
    But what is life—without a man ? "

PASTORAL SONG.

To the Tune of " The Yellow-hair'd Laddie."

IN May when the gowans appear on the green,
And flow'rs in the field and the forest are seen ;
Where lilies bloom'd bonny, and hawthorns upsprung,
The Yellow-hair'd laddie oft whistled and sung.

But neither the shades, nor the sweets of the flow'rs,
Nor the blackbirds that warbled on blossoming bow'rs,
Could pleasure his eye, or his ear entertain ;
For love was his pleasure, and love was his pain.

The shepherd thus sung, while his flocks all around
Drew nearer and nearer, and sigh'd to the sound :
Around as in chains, lay the beasts of the wood,
With pity disarmed, with music subdu'd.

Young Jessy is fair as the spring's early flower,
And Mary sings sweet as the bird in her bower :
But Peggy is fairer and sweeter than they ;
With looks like the morning, with smiles like the day.

In the flower of her youth, in the bloom of eighteen,
Of virtue the goddess, of beauty the queen :
One hour in her presence an æra excels
Amid courts, where ambition with misery dwells.

Fair to the shepherd the new-springing flow'rs,
When May and when morning lead on the gay hours :
But Peggy is brighter and fairer than they ;
She's fair as the morning, and lovely as May.

Sweet to the shepherd the wild woodland sound,
When larks sing above him, and lambs bleat around :
But Peggy far sweeter can speak and can sing,
Than the notes of the warblers that welcome the Spring.

When in beauty she moves by the brook of the plain,
You would call her a Venus new sprung from the main :
When she sings, and the woods with their echoes reply,
You would think that an angel was warbling on high.

Ye Pow'rs that preside over mortal estate !
Whose nod ruleth Nature, whose pleasure is fate,
O grant me, O grant me the heav'n of her charms !
May I live in her presence, and die in her arms !

LOCHLEVEN NO MORE.

To the Tune of " Lochaber no More."

FAREWELL to Lochleven and Gairney's fair stream :
How sweet, on its banks, of my Peggy to dream !
But now I must go to a far distant shore,
And I 'll maybe return to Lochleven no more.

No more in the Spring shall I walk with my dear,
Where gowans bloom bonny, and Gairney runs clear ;
Far hence must I wander, my pleasures are o'er,
Since I 'll see my dear maid and Lochleven no more.

No more do I sing, since far from my delight,
But in sighs spend the day, and in tears the long night ;
By Devon's dull current stretch'd mourning I 'll lie,
While the hills and the woods to my mourning reply.

But wherever I wander, by night or by day,
True love to my Peggy still with me shall stay ;
And ever and aye my loss I 'll deplore,
Till the woodlands re-echo Lochleven no more.

Though from her far distant, to her I 'll be true,
And still my fond heart keep her image in view :
O could I obtain her, my griefs were all o'er,
I would mourn the dear maid and Lochleven no more.

But if Fate has decreed that it ne'er shall be so,
Then grief shall attend me wherever I go ;
Till from life's stormy sea I reach death's silent shore,
Then I 'll think upon her and Lochleven no more.

SATIRES.

(FRAGMENT.)

I.

OR shall we weep, or grow into the spleen,
Or shall we laugh at the fantastic scene,
To see a dull mechanic, in a fit,
Throw down his plane, and strive to be a wit ?
Thus wrote De Foe, a tedious length of years,
And bravely lost his conscience and his ears,
To see a priest eke out the great design,
And tug with Latin points the halting line.
Who would not laugh, if two such men there were ?
Such there have been—I don't say such there are.

II.

" Last week I made a visit to Portmoak, the parish where
I was born, and being accidentally at the funeral of an
aged rustic, I was invited to partake of the usual entertain-
ment before the interment. We were conducted into a
large barn, and placed almost in a square,

When lo ! a mortal, bulky, grave, and dull.
The mighty master of the sevenfold skull,
Arose like Ajax. In the midst he stands—
A well filled bicker loads his trembling hands.
To one he comes, assumes a visage new—
" Come, ask a blessing, John ?—'tis put on you."
" Bid Mungo say," says John, with half a face,
Famed for his length of beard and length of grace.
Thus have I seen, beneath a hollow rock,
A shepherd hunt his dogs among his flock—
" Run, collie, Battie, Venture." Not one hears,
Then rising, runs himself, and running swears.

N

In short, sir, as I have not time to poetize, the grace is said, the drink goes round, the tobacco pipes are lighted, and, from a cloud of smoke, a hoary-headed rustic addressed the company thus:—"Weel, John (*i.e.*, the deceased), noo when he's gone, was a good, sensible man, stout, and healthy, and hale; and had the best hand for casting peats of onybody in this kintra side. Aweel, sirs, we maun a' dee—Here's to ye." I was struck with the speech of this honest man, especially with his heroic application of the glass, in dispelling the gloomy thoughts of death.

THE FALL OF THE TABLE, GAIRNEY BRIDGE,
JUNE, 1765 (*h*).

WITHIN this school a table once there stood—
It was not iron—No! 'twas rotten wood.
Four generations it on earth had seen—
A ship's old planks composed the huge machine.
Perhaps that ship in which Columbus hurl'd
Saw other stars rise on another world,—
Or that which bore, along the dark profound,
From pole to pole, the valiant Drake around.—
Tho' miracles were said long since to cease,
Three weeks—thrice seven long days—it stood in peace :
Upon the fourth, a warm debate arose,
Managed by words, and more emphatic blows ;
The routed party to the table fled,
Which seemed to offer a defensive shade.
Thus, in the town, I've seen, when rains descend,
When arched porticoes their shades extend,
Papists and gifted Quakers, Tories, Whigs,
Forget their feuds, and join to save their wigs—

Men born in India, men in Europe bred,
Commence acquaintance in a mason's shed.
Thus they ensconc'd beneath the table lay,—
With shouts the victors rush upon the prey,—
Attack'd the rampart where they shelter took.
With firing battered, and with engines shook,
It fell. The mighty ruins strew the ground.
It fell! The mountains tremble at the sound.
But to what end (say you) this trifling tale?
To tell you man as well as wood is frail;
Haste then since life can little more supply,
"Than just to look about us and to die."

ECLOGUE.

IN THE MANNER OF OSSIAN.

O COME, my love! from thy echoing hill; thy locks on the mountain wind!

The hill-top flames with setting light; the vale is bright with the beam of eve. Blithe on the village green the maiden milks her cows. The boy shouts in the wood, and wonders who talks from the trees. But Echo talks from the trees, repeating his notes of joy. Where art thou, O Morna! thou fairest among women? I hear not the bleating of thy flock, nor thy voice in the wind of the hill. Here is the field of our loves; now is the hour of thy promise. See, frequent from the harvest-field the reapers eye the setting sun: but thou appearest not on the plain.—

Daughters of the bow! Saw ye my love, with her little flock tripping before her? Saw ye her, fair moving over the heath, and waving her locks behind like the yellow sunbeams of evening?

Come from the hill of clouds, fair dweller of woody Lumon!

I was a boy when I went to Lumon's lovely vale. Sporting among the willows of the brook, I saw the daughters of the plain. Fair were their faces of youth; but mine eye was fixed on Morna. Red was her cheek, and fair her hair. Her hand was white as the lily. Mild was the beam of her blue eye, and lovely as the last smile of the sun. Her eye met mine in silence. Sweet were our words together in secret. I little knew what meant the heavings of my bosom, and the wild wish of my heart. I often looked back upon Lumon's vale, and blest the fair dwelling of Morna. Her name dwelt ever on my lip. She came to my dream by night. Thou didst come in thy beauty, O maid! lovely as the ghost of Malvina, when, clad with the robes of heaven, she came to the vale of the Moon, to visit the aged eyes of Ossian king of harps.

Come from the cloud of night, thou first of our maidens! come——

The wind is down; the sky is clear: red is the cloud of evening. In circles the bat wheels overhead; the boy pursues his flight. The farmer hails the signs of heaven, the promise of halcyon days: Joy brightens in his eyes. O Morna! first of maidens! thou art the joy of Salgar! thou art his one desire! I wait thy coming on the field. Mine eye is over all the plain. One echo spreads on every side. It is the shout of the shepherds folding their flocks. They call to their companions, each on his echoing hill. From the red cloud rises the evening star.—But who

comes yonder in light, like the Moon the queen of heaven ?
It is she! the star of stars! the lovely light of Lumon!
Welcome, fair beam of beauty, for ever to shine in our
valleys !

MORNA.

I come from the hill of clouds. Among the green rushes
of Balva's bank, I follow the steps of my beloved. The
foal in the meadow frolics round the mare : his bright
mane dances on the mountain wind. The leverets play
among the green ferns, fearless of the hunter's horn, and of
the bounding greyhound. The last strain is up in the
wood.—Did I hear the voice of my love ? It was the gale
that sports with the whirling leaf, and sighs in the reeds of
the lake. Blessed be the voice of winds that brings my
Salgar to mind. O Salgar! youth of the rolling eye! thou
art the love of maidens. Thy face is a sun to thy friends :
thy words are sweet as a song : thy steps are stately on
thy hill : thou art comely in the brightness of youth ; like
the Moon, when she puts off her dun robe in the sky, and
brightens the face of night. The clouds rejoice on either
side : the traveller in the narrow path beholds her, round,
in her beauty moving through the midst of heaven. Thou
art fair, O youth of the rolling eye! thou wast the love of
my youth.

SALGAR.

Fair wanderer of evening! pleasant be thy rest on our
plains. I was gathering nuts in the wood for my love, and
the days of our youth returned to mind ; when we played
together on the green, and flew over the field with feet of
wind. I tamed the blackbird for my love, and taught it to
sing in her hand. I climbed the ash in the cliff of the rock,
and brought you the doves of the wood.

MORNA.

It is the voice of my beloved! Let me behold him from the wood-covered vale, as he sings of the times of old, and complains to the voice of the rock. Pleasant were the days of our youth, like the songs of other years. Often have we sat on the old gray stone, and silent marked the stars, as one by one they stole into the sky. One was our wish by day, and one our dream by night.

SALGAR.

I found an apple-tree in the wood. I planted it in my garden. Thine eye beheld it all in flower. For every bloom we marked, I count an apple of gold. To-morrow I pull the fruit for you. O come, my best beloved.

MORNA.

When the gossamer melts in air, and the furze crackle in the beam of noon, O come to Cona's sunny side, and let thy flocks wander in our valleys. The heath is in flower. One tree rises in the midst. Sweet flows the river by its side of age. The wild bee hides his honey at its root. Our words will be sweet on the sunny hill. Till gray evening shadow the plain, I will sing to my well-beloved.

THE VANITY OF OUR DESIRE OF IMMORTALITY HERE:

A STORY IN THE EASTERN MANNER.

CHILD of the years to come, attend to the words of Calem;—Calem, who hath seen fourteen kings upon the throne of China, whose days are a thousand four hundred thirty and nine years.

Thou, O young man! who rejoicest in thy vigour; the days of my strength were as thine. My possessions were large, and fair as the gardens of Paradise. My cattle covered the valleys; and my flocks were as the grass on Mount Tirza. Gold was brought me from the ocean, and jewels from the Valley of Serpents. Yet I was unhappy: for I feared the sword of the angel of Death.

One day, as I was walking through the woods which grew around my palace, I heard the song of the birds: but I heard it without joy. On the contrary, their cheerfulness filled me with melancholy. I threw myself on a bank of flowers, and gave vent to my discontent in these words: "The time of the singing of birds is come, and the voice of the turtle is heard. These trees spread their verdant branches above me, and beneath the flowers bloom fair. The whole creation rejoices in its existence. I alone am unhappy. Why am I unhappy? What do I want? Nothing. But what avail my riches, when in a little I must leave them? What is the life of man? His days are but a thousand years! As the waves of the ocean; such are the generations of man: The foremost is dashed on the shore, and another comes rolling on. As the leaves of a tree; so are the children of men: They are scattered abroad by the wind, and other leaves lift their green heads. So, the generations before us are gone; this shall pass away, and another race arise. How, then, can I be glad, when in a few centuries I shall be no more? Thou Eternal, why hast thou cut off the life of man? and why are his days so few?"

I held my peace. Immediately the sky was black with the clouds of night. A tempest shook the trees of the forest: the thunder roared from the top of Tirza, and the red bolt shot through the darkness. Terror and amazement seized me ; and the hand of him before whom the sun is extinguished was upon me. "Calem," said he (while my bones trembled), "I have heard thee accusing me. Thou desirest life; enjoy it. I have commanded Death, that he touch thee not."

Again the clouds dispersed ; and the sun chased the shadows along the hills. The birds renewed their song sweeter than ever before I had heard them. I cast mine eyes over my fields, while my heart exulted with joy. "These," said I, "are mine for ever!" But I knew not that sorrow waited for me.

As I was returning home, I met the beautiful Selima walking across the fields. The rose blushed in her cheeks ; and her eyes were as the stars of the morning. Never before had I looked with a partial eye on woman. I gazed : I sighed; I trembled. I led her to my house, and made her mistress of my riches.

As the young plants grow up around the cedar ; so my children grew up in my hall.

Now my happiness was complete. My children married ; and I saw my descendants in the third generation. I expected to see them overspread the kingdom, and that I should obtain the crown of China.

I had now lived a thousand years ; and the hand of time had withered my strength. My wife, my sons, and my daughters, died ; and I was a stranger among my people. I was a burden to them ; they hated me, and drove me from my house. Naked and miserable, I wandered ; my tottering legs scarce supported my body. I went to the dwellings of my friends ; but they were gone, and other masters chid me from their doors. I retired to the woods :

and, in a cave, lived with the beasts of the earth. Berries and roots were my meat; and I drank of the stream of the rock. I was scorched with the summer's sun; and shivered in the cold of winter. I was weary of life.

One day I wandered from the woods, to view the palace which was once mine. I saw it; but it was low. Fire had consumed it: It lay as a rock cast down by an earthquake. Nettles sprung up in the court; and from within the owl scream'd hideous. The fox looked out at the windows: the rank grass of the wall waved around his head. I was filled with grief at the remembrance of what it, and what I had been. "Cursed be the day," I said, "in which I desired to live for ever. And why, O Thou Supreme! didst Thou grant my request? Had it not been for this, I had been at peace; I had been asleep in the quiet grave; I had not known the desolation of my inheritance; I had been free from the weariness of life. I seek for death, but I find it not: my life is a curse unto me."

A shining cloud descended on the trees; and Gabriel the angel stood before me. His voice was as the roaring stream, while thus he declared his message: "Thus saith the Highest, What shall I do unto thee, O Calem? What dost thou now desire? Thou askedst life, and I gave it thee, even to live for ever. Now thou art weary of living; and again thou hast opened thy mouth against me."

APPENDIX : NOTES TO THE POEMS.

Note (*a*) p. 77.

LOCHLEVEN—FIRST SKETCH.

WE agree with Dr MacKelvie's estimate of the following lines omitted in Logan's edition, but contained in the first draught of the Poem, in the MS. recovered by the father. "They are," he says, "more beautiful than some that have been retained." They come in immediately after the line—

> "The twining alders darken all the scene,"

and run thus—

> " Beneath their covert slept the ruffian wolf,
> And fox invidious, with the lesser brood
> That feed on life, or o'er the frighted wild
> Pursue the trembling prey. Here, too, unscathed
> By man, the graceful deer trip'd o'er the lawn,
> Nor heard the barking of the deep-mouthed hound,
> Nor sounding horn, nor feared the guileful net."

Note *b* p. 77.

LOCHLEVEN—EPISODE OF LEVINA.

As regards the episode of Levina, which makes up about two-fifths of the entire Poem, this has been claimed for Logan by his friends. Logan himself never claimed it publicly. He does not insert it among the poems printed in his own name in 1781, or indicate by any note in that volume a suppressed claim. Dr MacKelvie, who goes at some length into this question, has no doubt that Bruce wrote the episode. Both he and Dr Grosart lay stress upon the admitted fact that the germ of Levina was found in the Bruce MS. in the possession of the former when he edited the Poems. They maintain that the MS. was a first sketch of Lochleven, and that the finished Poem as it appeared in 1770 was the form it assumed when transcribed into the quarto volume.

That Bruce had in his estimation " finished " Lochleven, we find from his letter to Pearson, in December, 1766.[1] Logan, however, it seems, had in private conversation with his biographer claimed

1 See letter, p. 204.

the episode of Levina, as he did at the same time, and, as we may
say in the same breath, the Ode to the Cuckoo and the Ode to
Paoli. Dr R. Small is prepared to accept Logan's *ipse dixit* as so
far conclusive on the point. He is, indeed, careful to fortify his
position by declaring that Logan had no motive "to exert the
inventive faculty" about such a trifle as the episode ; which yet he
tells us makes up about two-fifths of the Poem, and is, he says,
distinguished from the rest of the piece by its finer imagery.

Dr Small, at the same time, knew well enough that Logan's
word was barely a sufficient warrant, and so he gives us some
confirmatory evidence. First then, in this chain of sequences,
there is, as we have said, Logan's guileless word, which there is no
reason to doubt. Then there is the supposed inability of Bruce,
in the short time at his disposal, from July to December of 1766 to
furnish, not what he admits is the germ of the episode, but its
appropriate development. In the last resort there are those
unfailing coincidences to which we have already had occasion to
refer in their character as evidence. There are, we are told,
expressions in Levina identical with others in Logan's Pastoral
Tale, showing a common parentage.

Such is the argument on which Dr Small rests the confident and
sweeping conclusion—"The love episode in 'Lochleven,' there is
no reason to doubt, is substantially Logan's."

Now it will be admitted that Logan's bare word is not proof.
As to Bruce not having time or strength to elaborate the episode,
this has more force ; but is, after all, a mere plausible conjecture.
The coincidences are, as Dr Small points out, very striking, and
would, as we have shown in another connection,[1] have strongly
supported his argument had Logan not taken into his custody, and
latterly destroyed, the quarto volume which might enable him, if
not "to repeat himself," at any rate consciously or unconsciously
to repeat and even transmute into what seemed his own characteristic phrases, the poetic vocabulary of Michael Bruce. Dr
MacKelvie goes farther than this, and draws down upon his head
the castigation of his critic for declaring as he does his firm
conviction that "The Pastoral Tale" where the chief coincidences
occur was the composition of Michael Bruce.

[1] See Writings, p. 41.

To conclude this discussion, if Dr Small could, indeed, prove that the recovered MS. was not a first sketch but the final and finished form of the Poem as it left the hand of Bruce ; then, on the shewing of Dr MacKelvie, it would follow that not only did Logan alter the episode of Levina, but also, and not less materially, the whole Poem.

In the absence of such proof, or of anything wearing the semblance of proof, we see no reason to doubt that the Poem of Lochleven, episode and all, as published in 1770, is substantially not the production of Logan, but of Michael Bruce.

Note (*c*) p. 90.

VISIT OF BRUCE TO ST. SERFS.

On the day before St. Luke's fair in Kinross I made a voyage to the Inch of Lochleven, that being the time at which, you know, they bring the cattle out of it. The middle and highest part of it is covered with ruins. The foundations are visible enough, and it seems to have been a very large building. The whole is divided into a great many little squares from which it appears not an unplausible conjecture that not only a church, as they tell us, but a monastery had stood on it. To the westward of this, and in the lower ground, a deep dyke in the form of a trench is cut in the north and east side of a plain piece of ground not unlike a bowling green. I can give no guess for the use of this, though it evidently appears to be a work of art. I sought among the ruins and the stones of the little house which stands on it for some marks of inscriptions, but to no purpose. I could find nothing further to assist my conjectures. I would have examined [word wanting in MS.] had not the fishers been in such a hurry to be gone.

They who consider it in no other view than as capable of feeding a dozen or fourteen cattle, when their work was over would not stay a minute longer had it been to discover the great toe of St. Moak who is buried there. My description of it in the Poem Lochleven, which by the way is now finished, runs thus—

Fronting where Gairny pours his silent urn, &c.

(Extract of letter from Michael Bruce to David Pearson, dated Dec., 1766.)

Note (*d*) p. 91.

SELMA.

Selma is Ossian's capital of Morven. This is the region of Celtic song. Here, Hugh Miller tells us, he began to tune his youthful lyre thus :—

> " Yes, oft I've said, as oft I've seen
> The men who dwell its hills among,
> That Morven's land has ever been
> A land of valour, worth, and song."

This is not the place to discuss the Ossian controversy, which exercised in no small degree the minds of some of our best literary men more than two generations ago, but was virtually settled by the committee of the Highland Society of Scotland, appointed to enquire into the nature and authenticity of the Poems of Ossian, and of which Henry MacKenzie was chairman. A full account of it will be found in the *Edinburgh Review* for 1805.

Note (*e*) p. 91.

LOCHLEVEN CASTLE.

Lochleven Castle, situated on an island, about half a mile from the Kinross shore, is said to have been founded by one of the Pictish kings, Congal, son of Dongart (511-535).

It was, from the first, the grand centre around which life in this quiet secluded region revolved. In peaceful times it was a favourite resort of kings and nobles, especially from the twelfth century onwards. Alexander III. lived for some time in it about 1256.

But storms, both by land and water, were wont to arise somewhat frequently around the castle and its environs. On these troublous occasions the castle fortress could well enough hold its own, as our southern foes again and again learned to their cost.

The siege of the castle in the time of Edward III (1334) by an English force under Sir John Strivelyn, has all the interest of a military romance. The little Scottish garrison not only held the fort, but sallied forth upon and routed the enemy.

For long continued generations the castle was used as one of our state prisons. Among the captives there confined we may mention such names as Robert II. and his son, " The Wolf of Badenoch,"

1268; Archibald, Earl of Douglas, 1429; Patrick Graham, Archbishop of St. Andrews; and last, as to order of time in our list, the Earl of Northumberland (1569). Most conspicuous of all is, we need not say, the Royal Prisoner of 1567, Mary Stuart, who was confined in the castle from the 16th June of that year until she escaped on May 2nd, 1568; only, however, to exchange Lochleven for Fotheringay.

We shall not venture upon the genealogies of the long list of Captains or even Lairds of Lochleven Castle. They were first scions of the noble house of Douglas, to one of whom, Sir Robert Douglas, James V. confirmed anew the rights of the proprietorship of the castle, and of the baronies of Kinross and Dalkeith. The estate, in due time, passed into the possession of their relations the Mortons, and they at last, towards the close of the 17th century, sold it to Sir William Bruce, in whose family it still remains; the present proprietor being Sir Graham Montgomery, who has done not a little to restore the castle and beautify its surroundings.

(See "Lochleven Castle and its Associations with Mary Queen of Scots," by R. Burns Begg, F.S.A., Scot. This is the standard popular work on the subject, written in a most engaging literary style, and full of new and interesting research.)

Note (*f*) p. 152.

INSCRIPTION ON BRUCE'S BIBLE.

The correct version of the Inscription, as given in the present text of the Poems, was, we believe, first published in the closing Article of an able and interesting series on Michael Bruce and his Writings in the *Kinross-shire Advertiser*, by Mr John G. Barnet, 1886.

Mr David Marshall assures me that he has seen the Bible in question, and so can verify the reading as it now stands.

The other version runs thus :—

> " 'Tis very vain for me to boast
> How small a price my Bible cost;
> The day of judgment will make clear
> 'Twas very cheap—or very dear."

Note (*g*) p. 119.

ODE TO THE CUCKOO.

We have given in the text the version of the Ode in the Miscellany, 1770. We now give it as it appeared in Logan's poems, 1781. The variations are indicated by italics.

ODE TO THE CUCKOO—(LOGAN, 1781).

HAIL, beauteous Stranger of *the grove !*
  Thou Messenger of Spring !
Now Heaven repairs thy rural seat,
  And woods thy welcome sing.

What time the daisy decks the green,
  Thy certain voice we hear ;
Hast thou a star to guide thy path,
  Or mark the rolling year ?

Delightful Visitant ! with thee
  I hail the time of flowers,
And hear the sound of music sweet
From birds among the bowers.

The school-boy, wandering thro' the wood
  To pull the *primrose* gay,
Starts, *the new* voice *of Spring* to hear,
  And imitates thy lay.

What time the pea puts on the bloom
  Thou fliest thy vocal vale,
An annual guest in other lands,
  Another Spring to hail.

Sweet Bird ! thy bower is ever green,
  Thy sky is ever clear ;
Thou hast no sorrow in thy song,
  No winter in thy year !

O could I fly, I'd fly with thee !
  We'd make, with *joyful* wing,
Our annual visit o'er the globe,
  Companions of the Spring.

Note (*h*) p. 194.

MICHAEL BRUCE, THE POET STUDENT, AND HIS COTTAGE SCHOOL AT GAIRNEY BRIDGE.

The following valuable communication, addressed to me, on the above subject, will explain itself.

Lochleven Place,
Kinross, 7th Aug., 1895.

Dear Sir,

    Referring to your visit to me yesterday, I did not recollect till you were gone that Robert Heron in his observations made in a journey through the western counties of Scotland in the autumn of 1792, has a paragraph on our darling poet, beginning, "About three miles south from Kinross stands the house which has been celebrated in a fine paper in the *Mirrour*, as the residence of the late Michael Bruce, an amiable young man of no mean poetical powers."

This ought, I think, to remove any doubt in your mind that Gairney Bridge, and not Bruce's birthplace at Kinnesswood, was meant by Lord Craig, when he wrote his touching tribute to the genius and virtue of our poet in 1779.

In addition to this, we have the testimony of James Kennedy, a native of Kinross-shire, who knew the house at Gairney Bridge celebrated by Lord Craig, and states in a note to his poem of Glenochel, published in 1810, that in passing between Kinross and Edinburgh in July, 1809, he stopped at Gairney Bridge (after an absence of several years) to look on the house of which the gentle Bruce had once been an inhabitant, but saw only the site, the house having been removed some time previously. In an article forming part of my unpublished "History of Kinross-shire and its people," entitled "Michael Bruce, the poet student, and his cottage school at Gairney Bridge," I have said, after giving all the evidence in detail: "The result of this inquiry shows that there were two houses at Gairney Bridge associated with Michael Bruce; one where he lived and slept, occasionally at least, which was in the village on the south side of the water, and was removed before July, 1809; the other on the north side of the Gairney, in the parish of Kinross, the old dwelling-house of Gairney Bridge End (now Gairney bank—then held by the same family, Mr John Bennet, and his aunt Anne Bennet—of which a fragment remains in the north wall of the garden, and a lintel preserved in a byre on the north side of the steading, with the date, 1675), used by the poet as a school, demolished in 1822."

Yours faithfully,

DAVID MARSHALL, F.S.A., Scot.